Short Shorts

Volume 2

Three One-Act Plays
by Michael Yates

Nettle Books

Short Shorts

Published 2014 by Nettle Books

nettlebooks@hotmail.co.uk

www.nettlebooks.weebly.com

www.michael-yates.co.uk

ISBN: 978-0-9561513-5-3

Classification: Drama

This book is dedicated to Tracey Yates, who drew the cover illustration.

Making a Drama Out of Life (Part Two)

As I wrote in Volume One of *Short Shorts*, my first stage play was the full-length and full-blown *Pontefractions*, a satirical history of the Yorkshire town of Pontefract. Afterwards, members of the cast told me they were eager to do more. *Did I have another play*? they asked.

And the answer was: *No, I didn't*. What I *did* have was a short story *QWERTYUIOP*, named after the keyboard and published in an anthology called *Yorkshire Mixture*. This comedy-drama was another historical work: the story of unemployed women taking a shorthand/typing course in Thatcher's Britain. The very intelligent but rather prim middle-class Susan discovers how little she really knows about life when she is plunged into the working-class milieu of the course. In the original story, a lot of the action is really the *re*action inside Susan's head; for the stage drama, I took a minor character, the sexy Frankie, and made her into Susan's lippy antagonist and nemesis and she steals the show.

And then came *The Navigator's Daughter*, the love/hate relationship of a mother and child.

And then came the play which begins this volume – my first one-act play *A Real Cushy Number*, based on my youthful experience of being a hospital porter.

As well as my day job as a newspaper journalist, I became during this period Poet in Residence in Whitby, in Wakefield Hospitals and at Wakefield Cathedral. I produced a number of short stories. But I seemed to have lost the theatrical touch. Until, as I wrote in Volume One, I met up with fellow writer Helen Shay and we co-operated on a series of dramatic double bills.

3

Ironically, the second play in this book, *All Good Men*, was not one of these. This saga of party politics, where the jokes more or less wrote themselves, was produced by Colin Lewisohn's Encore Theatre group as a companion piece to Colin's own play *Sex and Politics*.

In 2011 I saw another of my full-length plays performed: *The Bronte Boy* is the tragic story of Branwell and was selected for Wakefield Drama Festival. And last year a new production was commissioned by the Bronte Society for their international AGM weekend at Haworth. Earlier, my play for children, *The Lightning Conductor*, was commissioned by a West Yorkshire school. And I also co-wrote *Doublecross*, a modern morality tale, with the aforementioned Helen.

The third play in this book is *Luvvies*. It began as a 30-minute two-hander in which a writer and an actress harangue the audience. But I knew it wasn't good enough and I finally re-wrote and enlarged it, introducing two new characters: now the nasty couple had a second couple to persecute.

If a full-length play is like a novel, branching out in many directions, the one-act play is a short story: linear, fast-paced and leading to a vivid climax. But the climaxes in this volume are often strange: the first play ends with a man stepping on a woodlouse; the second with a guilty couple between the sheets; while the third ends with another couple planning an escape by taxi. I hope you enjoy all of them.

Michael Yates 2014

Contents

A Real Cushy Number

...is a tale of good and evil, played out in a hospital porters' room on a late shift when the porters and a visiting priest are awaiting the death of an accident victim. It was premiered at Featherstone Community Theatre in 1998 and performed by the aptly-named One-off Productions as part of a double bill called *Small Miracles*. Cast and crew:

Mr Bunting... Andrew Reece
Wal... Ron Corn
Father Desmond..................................... Gary Stephenson
Billy.. John Wadsworth

Directed by John Wadsworth
Length: 30 minutes

Characters:

Mr Bunting: Head porter at the hospital. About 60 years old. Speaks in a working class accent but in a self-conscious sermonising style, full of repetition.

Wal: A hospital porter, middle-aged-to-elderly. Working class with no frills and no apologies.

Fr Desmond: A Catholic priest about the same age as Wal, intelligent, ironically humorous, amiable, but weak and aware of his weakness. He likes Wal, and enjoys his intellectual challenge.

Billy: A hospital porter of indeterminate age. He has only a handful of lines and is really a plot device to provide an ending.

Scene: The porters' room at a major English hospital.

Time: The present; late night / early hours of a winter's day

Furniture: Three wooden chairs. A small table.

Props: A kettle, three tea mugs, a packet of tea, a half-empty bottle of milk, a copy of *The Sun*.

Costume: The three porters should wear identical shirts and identical trousers. Each should have a key chain attached to his belt and the (supposed) keys in the back pocket of his trousers. The priest wears a black suit and shirt with a clerical collar.

Sound effects: An ambulance siren. The flushing of a toilet (twice). A piercing scream.

Lighting: Very basic to indicate indoors late at night. No changes of mood.

SOUND OF AMBULANCE SIREN. IT FADES.
LIGHTS GO UP ON THREE WOODEN CHAIRS
COVERED WITH THROWS AND AN ELECTRIC
KETTLE ON A SMALL TABLE AT THE BACK. A
COPY OF THE SUN LIES ON THE FLOOR. THERE
ARE THREE PEOPLE IN THE ROOM: FR
DESMOND, MR BUNTING AND WAL. FR
DESMOND SITS ON THE CHAIR STAGE RIGHT,
MR BUNTING ON ITS TWIN STAGE LEFT. WAL
SITS ON THE THIRD CHAIR CENTRE BACK. ALL
THREE HAVE MUGS IN THEIR HANDS AND ARE
DRINKING TEA. WAL'S MUG HAS A NAKED
WOMAN PAINTED ON IT.

WAL: (BREAKING THE SILENCE,
            AND TO NO–ONE IN PARTICULAR) Roll on
            death! Who'd work in an 'ospital? (THEN,
            QUICKLY, TO FR DESMOND) Sorry, Padre –
            wasn't thinking. (HE TAKES ANOTHER
            GULP OF TEA)

MR BUNTING: (SHARPLY) You've no
            feelings, Wal, none at all. I'm surprised at you.
            (THEN, CHANGING THE TONE OF HIS
            VOICE AND ADDRESSING FR DESMOND)
            Anyway, as I was saying, Father, it's a lot colder
            tonight than it was last night. I don't normally do
            nights, me being head porter like. (HE
            INDICATES A SMALL BADGE ON HIS
            SHIRT) They don't expect me to do it. Mr
            Bunting, they say, we don't expect a man of
            your seniority to do nights. But with Chopdat
            away, he's my night foreman, well, I had to do
            it. Gunga Din, that's what I call 'im. Says he's
            got a cold id de nose, Asian flu (LOOKS
            ROUND FOR APPRECIATION AND
            LAUGHS AT OWN JOKE) that sort of thing.
            Well, I've heard that sort of excuse before. And
            I'll not stand for it, the men know I won't! I'll

'ave 'im when he gets back. *Chopdat*, I'll say, *don't give me your flu! You've 'ad a drop too much, a night on the town, that's why you couldn't come in. Don't think I don't know*! Oh it drives him mad, that sort of talk, him being strict Muslim and all. Oh, he'll wave his hands and roll his eyes, the way they do, and I'll say *all right, all right* and calm him down. *All right, all right,* I'll say, but I'll give a wink to the rest of the men, show what my true feelings are, Well, you've got to be honest in *my* job else the men won't respect you. (BEAT) Still, nothing else I could do for now. So that's why I'm doing nights, Father. That's the only reason. (RAISES HIS VOICE, STARTS TO INCLUDE WAL IN THE CONVERSATION) Though I don't know why I didn't do it before, seein' as how it's a right cushy number, just drinkin' tea all night. Once the pubs is shut and the knife fights and the road crash cases is in. And they're all done by midnight. Well, nothing to do then except make a cup of tea, eh Wal? You should've made one for Billy. We could give it him if we knew where he was. It's fifteen minutes since I sent him round the wards. He'll be chatting up one of them West Indian nurses on geriatrics, I know he will. Gives us all a bad name then. I could find him things to do. I know his job, you see, I know them all. I've done them all. That's why they made me head porter.

FR DESMOND: (COMING OUT OF HIS REVERIE) What? What was it you said about death, Wal? I missed that.

MR BUNTING: (to FR DESMOND) Don't pay him no heed. (HE LAUGHS)

FR DESMOND: (HE NODS, PUTS HIS EMPTY MUG DOWN ON THE FLOOR) You make a good cup of tea, Wal. I asked the parents did they want one, but they said not. (HE LOOKS OFF INTO THE MIDDLE DISTANCE AND BEGINS TO TALK TO NO–ONE IN PARTICULAR) That boy of theirs – God knows his heart is still beating. I performed the last rites an hour ago. A double decker bus hits his motorbike head on and he's still with us – just. And those two outside, up there on the ward, his mam and dad, (HE WAVES AN ARM TOWARDS A REGION OFFSTAGE) they just sit there. Her with her hair in curlers, would you believe? I didn't think women used them any more. And him with his glasses, big thick glasses with circles in the lenses, great thick things, round and round, he mustn't be able to see an arm's length without 'em, that's for sure. Huddled in their overcoats on those damn metal chairs, just watching him, watching that boy of theirs. I suppose I should have stayed with them to offer comfort but I can't stand those chairs. (STARTS TO ADDRESS THE OTHERS ONCE MORE) I said to them to come down here, get a bit of warmth, but they want to be with him. Right to the end. I had to get away. Those bloody chairs! Canvas and steel! I do my best, Wal, but the flesh is weak – particularly the flesh on me arse.

WAL: I dunno why they bother, these doctors. Keeping him hanging on. Did you see his head when they brought him in? Squashed tomatoes. When they took him out of the ambulance, I swear Billy stuck his fingers through it. All red his fingers was. He went right out and washed his hands afterwards. He's very clean is Billy. (PUTS MUG DOWN AND

GESTURES WITH HIS HANDS) Let him go,
why can't they? Put him out of his misery. Give
it a rest. Give us all a rest.

FR DESMOND: It's not for us to decide, Wal.
That's what we have God for.

MR BUNTING: He giveth and 'e taketh away.
Bit too strong for me, Wal, as a matter of fact.
Could've done with more milk. (PUTS HIS CUP
DOWN NEXT TO FR DESMOND'S)

WAL: (HE GETS UP SUDDENLY,
STAMPS FOOT ON FLOOR AS THOUGH
CRUSHING AN INSECT) Bloody woodlouse!
(SITS DOWN AGAIN AND GLANCES AT
HIS WATCH) Another two hours for you and
me, Mr Bunting, another two hours before the
day shift. But Fr Desmond here could be stuck
for half the day. And for what? He was as good
as dead when he come in, Father. Why prolong
the misery? Don't tell me you're hoping for a
miracle? I don't believe in 'em.

MR BUNTING: (TO FR DESMOND) He don't
mean that, of course. I'm a lay preacher, meself,
Father. I don't know if you know that. The
United Church of Zion on Golden Hillock Road.
I can bear witness to miracles, oh yes, in me own
life as well as those of ordinary people.

FR DESMOND: (TO WAL) Depends what you
call miracles, Wal. You and me sitting here,
talking like this, is this not a miracle? OK, it's a
cliché – but all life is a miracle, something
made from nothing. That's what we are. That's
what that boy upstairs is, squashed tomatoes or
no squashed tomatoes.

11

MR BUNTING: (WARMING UP) Oh, I could tell you about miracles. I could tell you…

FR DESMOND: (INTERRUPTING) And I'll tell you another miracle, Wal: the mercy of Jesus Christ. That's one miracle those poor people upstairs still believe in, those poor benighted parents, and their poor dying son on his cut-price 250cc. It's the only thing that saves them from despair.

MR BUNTING: That's it! That's it exactly! You should listen to 'im, Wal. Listen to Father Desmond – he's an educated man! And you should listen to *me* an 'all. Oh, I could tell you stories about miracles!

WAL: That's as may be, but I don't believe in miracles and I don't believe in God. Tell you what I do believe in though – reincarnation. Ever since I was a nipper, six years old, and I watched this Laurel and Hardy film and right at the end Ollie gets killed an' comes back as a donkey. And there he is in a field eating grass and wearing a straw hat and Stan still recognises him! Yes, I've always believed in reincarnation. Ever since that film. I sometimes look at people and I think: Wonder what he'll come back as? Mind you, with some of 'em I just look and I can tell *exactly* what they'll be. (BEAT) Anyway, miracles. I'll tell you both a little story. After all, we've got plenty of time and nothing to do, like Mr Bunting was saying. I'll just tell it like it happened, because it's a true story, and you tell us what you make of it. (HE WIPES HIS MOUTH WITH HIS FINGERS)

MR BUNTING: I 'ope it's not a dirty story, Wal. We don't want none of your filth at this time of night. Don't forget who we've got with us…

WAL: I don't think Fr Desmond is going to worry, Mr Bunting. It's not a dirty story at all, Father.

FR DESMOND: I'm sure it's not, Wal.

WAL: Well, when I come out of the army, there was this bloke called Tommy Keene, a mucker of mine. He was an 'ard case, was Tommy. Drop you soon as look at you. But funnily enough, him and me got on. I was a bit of a tearaway meself in them days. We used to get pissed and pick up tarts together. (MR BUNTING TUT–TUTS IN DISGUST AT THIS REVELATION, FR DESMOND SMILES) One day Tommy went off for two weeks' holiday in Belgium and he went and married this Belgian girl and brought her back to live with 'is mom and dad. Cecile, her name was, but everybody round where he lived called her Cicely. He was really stuck on this Cicely, never raised a finger to 'er like I seen him do to some tarts.

FR DESMOND: The healing power of a good woman's love. Well, that's a miracle for a start, Wal. And I've seen it many times myself.

MR BUNTING: Oh, I don't know about that, Father. I don't much hold with women being able to do a man good. I don't see why God should give them such power. I mean, special women, exceptional women, women like Mother Teresa, well, there you've got a point, I don't doubt it. But your ordinary woman, your average common–or–garden, specially the women they

13

get round here, well, I would think it was more than a miracle if one of them did *me* any good. I don't know about you, Father, but I am constantly warning young men about the snares of young women, which have grown in our time, Father, grown like the very Leviathan, if it's my opinion you're after. But the young men don't listen, of course…

WAL: It was Tommy that got me this job down the Nissan. That's when I lived in Birmingham. We was on the track. It was good money for them days, but it was all nights and it made you mad with boredom. God knows, this job can be bad enough. I've seen men lose their marbles right here in this room. Like Plaskett, the kitchen porter. When we changed the lockers round, when we moved them from this wall here (WAVES HAND) to that one round the corner, one of Mr Bunting's reorganisations, old Plaskett just comes in as usual and stands here turning his locker key round and round in the empty wall. You can still see the mark. We took half an hour to explain to him that we'd moved the lockers. (BEAT) But this is nothing like that car factory. Not for driving you mad.

MR BUNTING: Course, it's all changed these days. Car factories. All robots these days. Not like in your time, Wal.

WAL: Even in my time it was robots, but the robots was people. People like me. (BEAT) Now, the parts came along the track and you picked 'em up and you got a can of this glue and you stuck 'em together and you put 'em down again and you started on the next lot and you picked 'em up and you stuck 'em together and you put 'em down again for hours at a stretch. It was blue murder. It made everybody mad, like bloody zombies…

MR BUNTING: Now, Wal…

WAL: I don't think zombies is a dirty word, Mr Bunting.

MR BUNTING: But we can do without the *bloody*. I think we'd all agree that if you've got something to say that's worth hearing, it doesn't need a *bloody* tacked on. I would say that's a golden rule, always true no matter what the circumstance. Stick by them golden rules, Wal, and you'll find people will listen to you with more respect.

WAL: Nobody would talk for hours on end, then they'd 'ave their little burst of fun. Now *that's* a golden rule, I always say. People have got to have their bit of fun. If they don't get allowed their bit of fun, there's no telling what could happen. I'll tell you what I mean…There used to be a supervisor called Menzies who was a bit of a nancy boy.

MR BUNTING: Wal…

FR DESMOND: It's allright, Mr Bunting. I've heard the term before. Even applied to men of the cloth.

WAL: This Menzies, we used to spit tea on 'is overall. We used to spit tea on him from behind and then he'd turn around and we'd all look up at the roof (HOLDS OUT HIS HAND) and say: *Oh dear, Mr Menzies, there must be a leak in that roof, and the rain's coming in. Maybe you better report that, Mr*

Menzies... And some of 'em used to hold 'im down and pull his trousers off. This Menzies didn't mind. He liked it. *Careful, lads – don't get me underpants dirty* – that's what he used to say. I can hear 'im now, daft bugger... And we used to set the track on fire when we was really bored. Because this glue we used, it was inflammable, it went up like a Roman Candle if you set a match to it. We used to set the track on fire or stick nuts and bolts into it to make it break down. We used to pray for that track to break down or for somebody to drop down dead. Now that *would* have been a miracle to us, it would... There was always cans of this glue around, very inflammable, and you'd light a cigarette and drop the match in some fella's glue, and it'd flare right up.

WAL GETS UP, CARRIES HIS MUG OVER TO THE KETTLE, MAKES HIMSELF ANOTHER CUP

MR BUNTING: The Devil makes work for idle hands. It's an old saying, Father, but it's the Gospel truth. I've seen the Devil, seen him meself, seen him as real as you or me.

WAL: (RETURNING TO SIT DOWN) Anyway, it ended up with some bugger setting fire to this Menzies' overall and they 'ad to call an ambulance. His legs was all burnt, and his hands where he tried to put it out. Nobody meant it to happen, but everybody was mad, everybody was zombies...

MR BUNTING: Wicked. A wicked act. (HE LOOKS TO FR DESMOND FOR CONFIRMATION) I hope there's a purpose in this story, Wal, I hope there's a moral. Because I think the recounting of wickedness for its own sake is as wicked as the wickedness recounted. It can have an evil effect. I've seen the evil effect of wickedness recounted, I've seen grown men turn to wickedness from the recounting of it.

FR DESMOND: Oh, I'm sure there's a moral. I'd stake my life on it.

WAL: It don't end there. Two days later, this Menzies chokes it in hospital. Delayed shock or summat. Then there's coppers all over the place taking statements. Foreman got the push for letting it 'appen. But they never found out who it was lit the match. Everybody was on to this Menzies, pulling at 'im, so nobody saw. Or if they did, they kept their trap shut. In the end, the coppers went home, the fuss died down, and there was still that bleedin' track. Still that bleedin' track and them bleedin' zombies.

MR BUNTING: The word bloody and the word bleedin' are equally unnecessary, Wal. Just by putting *ing* on the end doesn't make it any more acceptable.

WAL: (IGNORING HIM) When I was saying about Tommy, I didn't mention how Cicely was havin' Tommy's kid and she 'ad a lot of bother. She kept on bleeding – there I can use *bleeding* like that, can't I, Mr Bunting? I mean I'm talking here about *real* bleeding, about blood coming out, gushing out...

MR BUNTING: If you must, Wal, if you must talk about bleeding in any shape or form...

FR DESMOND: But if there's a moral, Mr Bunting, if there's a purpose to the story, then I think we should allow him to say it.

MR BUNTING: Very well, Father, you're an educated man, you know about these things.

WAL: And 'er and Tommy kept thinkin' they was gonna lose it. They thought they was gonna lose the baby. In the end, the doctors took 'er in to hospital, a bit like this one I shouldn't wonder, and she's got to just lie there, week in, week out, can't do nothing, can't read a library book – and she was one for reading was Cicely, though she had to read in French of course because her English was OK for talking but not good enough for reading library books. No, she can't 'ardly sit up for fear of hurting the kid. And all this time, Tommy's boozing his head off.

MR BUNTING: He should be ashamed. But I blame her in part for marrying a man like that.

WAL: Then the thing with Menzies 'appened and Tommy just walked out. *I've 'ad about enough,* he says, *I can't work no more, I've got to be with Cicely.* So they give 'im 'is cards and I don't see 'im for, oh, about six month or more. When I do, it's on a 156 bus and he's the conductor. Well, he was so glad to see me, he let me ride for free, but he said he'd have to take me money if the inspector got on…

MR BUNTING: Even a common-or-garden omnibus can easily become the vehicle of unrighteousness.

WAL: It turns out he's been doing this bus job regular for three months and 'e says why don't I go round and see the family some time? Him and Cicely and the kid 'ave got theirselves

18

a council 'ouse by now. Before, they used to live with his mother and she wasn't the easiest person to get on with, I can tell you stories…

MR BUNTING: I'm surprised at that. Mothers are the best of women as a general rule, as far as women go. In fact, I don't mind saying that mothers – if they're past a certain age or at least can act in accordance with the idea of being so – can be a good influence on a man. A veritable source of light. My own mother was a case in point…

WAL: So I go round one Sunday morning and we go down the pub. And 'e's changed right enough, has Tommy, off the beer for a start, the lemonade kid. And he's not lookin' over 'is shoulder for somebody to put one on. You've changed, I says. That I 'ave, he says, I've been to church this morning, and it wouldn't do you no 'arm to pop in there now and again, Wal… Well, I'm not daft, and I've got a shrewd idea as to how it's all come about…

FR DESMOND: Our friend Mr Menzies.

MR BUNTING: Oh, yes, him that got burned.

WAL: And in the end he tells me: *It was me as killed that poor bugger, Wal. It would serve me right if God struck me and mine dead. But 'e hasn't. He's give me a second chance.* I have a think about that. *The kid,* I says. *The kid,* he says, *She nearly lost it, but I prayed and prayed, first time since I was a kid meself. Don't let it die, I said, don't let her die neither! I swore I'd change if me prayers was answered, Wal….* Well, I've not seen Tommy in years now. I wouldn't know what to say to 'im if I saw 'im in the street. But I'm told he's got two more kids and he's something like assistant chief inspector or one of these fancy names they give theirselves. Owns his own house too.

MR BUNTING: Owns his own house! God works in mysterious ways. He strikes down the pervert and guides the prodigal back to the path of righteousness e'en for his own name's sake. Isn't that true, Father?

FR DESMOND: It's true enough. But that's not the end of it. Am I right, Wal?

WAL: You're right. Oh yes, you're right, Padre. I can see you don't miss a trick. (HE SMILES) The kid was asleep that morning when I went round. But when we went back for dinner, Cicely was changing it. A big kid it was, very quiet, not moving much. When I got a good look at it, the big 'ead and the funny eyes... It was a dead ringer for the kid my Aunt Dorothy had. A mongol, that's what it was, what they call Down's Syndrome these days. But big words or no, that's what it was.

FR DESMOND: And they knew?

WAL: Knew from the day it was born.

FR DESMOND: Ahh. (HE BITES HIS LIP) You know, Wal, sometimes I feel like a man with a newspaper crossword that I do every day, and I'm always looking to see into the mind of the man who compiles it. And there I am, trying to recognise the man behind it, so then I know how it all works, I can see the pattern of his thought behind the clues. You see, I'm always teaching that God is infinite in his wisdom and in his goodness too. Now – a miracle or a punishment? Absolution or abandonment? Proof of heaven or hell on earth? That's what he's asking us, Mr Bunting. They've got their baby, they've got their lives, the sins of the past are in the past. But… a suspicion lingers. It's a good story, Wal, a sly one. But I've no simple answer. (HE TRAILS OFF, SMILES WITH SELF DEPRECATION. WAL GRINS.)

MR BUNTING: (QUICKLY) Of course you've got an answer, Father. Same as the answer I'd give any day. .. Miracles! I've no doubts about miracles. I'm living proof meself. I was like you once upon a time, Wal, I didn't believe. Nearly broke me mother's heart with me gallivanting and not following the ways of the Lord. Oh, I remember my mother in her black dress, at my Father's funeral. Wonderful woman. And a black hat with a veil, a thing you don't see on women nowadays. Oh, a woman in a smart dress and a hat with a veil is a thing of beauty, priced above rubies. But a woman without 'er clothes, a woman that shows her body… this sort of filth! (PICKS UP THE COPY OF THE SUN) Oh, I wouldn't give you tuppence in the old money. (THROWS PAPER DOWN) The love between men and women, it isn't all this carnal stuff that's so fashionable nowadays. Oh no. That's not what the Bible means when it says he had knowledge of her. No, people may say it is, but let me tell you – the English language hasn't changed so much since Biblical times… You know, it's more than 15 years since I've seen my wife in a state of nakedness and I've not felt deprived. Because marriage is based on something more than that sort of thing. It's based on our love of the Lord. If we love Him,

then He loves us. We've got the miracle of
God's love, oh yes. The Lord provides. *Take
therefore no thought for the morrow...* That's
what I'm always saying to the others down at
chapel and I'm always proved right. Our pastor,
Mr Robinson, said it to me only the other day.
Mr Bunting, he says, *you've been proved right
again,* he says. *You don't 'ave to tell me, pastor,*
I says. And Mr Robinson's an educated man.
Take the building fund. How long is it now? Six
years we've been raising money for a new
chapel with a bit of an 'all to one side where we
can take our tea and hold our jumble sales. *We'll
never make the target at this rate, Mr Bunting,*
says the pastor. *Fear not,* I says, *only trust in the
Lord.* And now this Mrs Hastings from Clayton
Street, she only goes an' dies an' leaves us
thousands! *You were right all along,* says Mr
Robinson. *Don't I know it!* I says. Oh yes,
miracles are things that happen every day if you
only know where to look. It's faith that makes
miracles. It was faith that made me visit Mrs
Hastings once she'd had her stroke. I met 'er
here, you know. Met 'er on the wards. And then
I seen her in out–patients two or three times.
And she was grateful. Grateful for the company
and for the word of the Lord which I brought 'er.
And I used to tell 'er about chapel, how we all
remembered 'er in our prayers, though most of
the people there didn't even know 'er, but I told
them about 'er. And I told 'er how we prayed for
new surroundings, for some concrete and
reinforced glass to stop the vandals. I told 'er
how, when it was time to meet the Lord face to
face, we all of us had to put our lives in order.
She was comforted by my words, I could see
that. She used to dribble out the side of 'er
mouth and I used to dab it with a tissue that I'd
bought meself. So that was a miracle. Two

miracles really. We got our money and another
soul was plucked like a brand from the burning.
Praise be to God!

FR DESMOND: (IRONICAL) Indeed.

WAL: What about you, Father? You
        got a story to tell about miracles?

FR DESMOND: Not as good as yours, Wal.

MR BUNTING: Now don't go annoying the
        Father, Wal. He didn't come here to tell us
        stories.

WAL: It passes the time though. Don't
        it pass the time, Padre?

MR BUNTING: If it's passing the time that
        bothers you, Wal, I can see this whole shift has
        got too easy. I can see it needs a few more added
        duties. There's certainly plenty as could be done
        on this shift which normally gets left for the lads
        in the morning. A bit of mopping, for instance.
        A bit of sweeping up. Oh, them idle hands, Wal,
        they are the devil's playground, and no mistake.

FR DESMOND: Allright, Wal, I've got a story.
        And I think it has a moral. And I think it has a
        point. Just like I think life has a point.

MR BUNTING: You listen, Wal, you listen to
        what Fr Desmond is saying. He's an educated
        man.

WAL: Hang on a minute, Padre. I
        gotta run to the lavatory. (HE SPRINGS TO HIS
        FEET AND SAYS TO MR BUNTING) It's all
        this tea.

MR BUNTING: Too much tea on this shift, I can see, too much time to drink it.

WAL: I just want to be comfortable to give Fr Desmond the attention he deserves.

FR DESMOND: I'm sure you do, Wal.

WAL LOOKS DOWN AT FLOOR, STAMPS ON ANOTHER WOODLOUSE, THEN EXITS STAGE LEFT, RUNNING

MR BUNTING: (TO FR DESMOND IN CONSPIRATORIAL TONES) I said I was surprised. Earlier on. I said I was surprised that he had no feelings, that Wal. But I'm not surprised. Not really. I know him, you see, I know 'em all, all the porters that've worked here the last... oh, 18 years. Some real head cases, some of them. Wal is the longest serving porter since Mickey Parrish the lift porter died and he could have been head porter in his day but some people just aren't cut out for leadership, are they, Father? Maybe they haven't got the education or the way of talking. (BEAT) Anyway, Wal was approached, I don't say he wasn't approached, but he decided it wasn't worth the extra money. Anyway, he prefers nights, likes to get away from the wife, read the racing paper, talk about the geegees with Billy. Oh yes, they like a bit of a flutter, the lads on this shift, and I know the bloke that puts on the bets for them. They think I don't but I do. This bloke works over at The Shakespeare, that pub on Riddings Road.

FR DESMOND: I believe I know the one.

MR BUNTING: They get the odd bottle of Guinness brought in from there before closing time because Chopdat doesn't mind if the rules get bent once in a while, even if he is a devout Muslim. Or *says* he is. (LAUGHS) And that's another reason Wal's drinking so much tea tonight, Father, because *I'm* here instead of Chopdat and he knows *I* don't allow the bringing-in of intoxicants. (SOUND OF THE TOILET FLUSHING) Hang on, he's on his way back.

WAL: (ENTERING, DOING UP FLY) I've got meself comfortable now, Padre. I'm all ears. (SITS DOWN)

FR DESMOND: OK. I don't know if this one's as subtle as yours, Wal. But I'm only a parish priest so you'll have to forgive me if it's not up to scratch. (TO MR BUNTING) Though it was actually told me by a monsignor. (TO BOTH OF THEM) Well, it seems there's this old man who's been coming into church every week for God knows how long. And for years before that, his wife would come in with him. And years before that, his daughter and his son. It seems the son was the first to go, I mean the first to lose his faith...

MR BUNTING: It's always the young men. And it's the snares of young women that does it.

FR DESMOND: But also the young man died. After losing his faith, the young man was killed in a road accident. He was buried in the church anyway because he returned to the faith during his time in hospital...

MR BUNTING: The Almighty works in mysterious ways...

FR DESMOND: There were witnesses, it seemed, the father and the mother and the sister, who said he asked for last rites and confession. Well, nobody could get out to him before he died, but the last rites were performed anyway.

WAL: And then the sister. You lost the sister.

FR DESMOND: You're not slow, Wal. Yes, we lost the sister. She lost her faith and stopped coming. Well, she lost *this* faith anyway. As a matter of fact, she married an Anglican and started worshipping with *them*. Every Sunday, regular as clockwork. Only *our* church, the church of her mother and father, never saw her again.

WAL: But not so bad. Not so far away.

FR DESMOND: You'd be surprised how some people regard that, Wal. I have to say there was bitterness. I don't mean in the church, I mean in the family. There was a rift between the parents and the daughter. And then the mother became very ill and I don't doubt the rift with the daughter had something to do with it. She developed a cancer. Somewhere in the stomach, the pancreas I think, I'm not an anatomical expert. She stopped coming to church as well. But the old man carried on. Except... when his wife stopped coming, he stopped taking communion.

WAL: Oh. Then what's the point of going?

FR DESMOND: What's the point indeed? But
          we get plenty of them, these half-way people.
          Some have lost their faith and are trying to get it
          back by a sort of…osmosis. You know, they
          think if they come to Mass then maybe it will all
          hang together again, become real again, maybe
          the faith will seep back into their bones. And we
          get others, people who have done some terrible
          wrong, or *think* they've done some terrible
          wrong, and don't feel worthy any more of God's
          love, which is a form of despair, the biggest sin
          of all in a faith that preaches forgiveness. And
          they, well, they come to remind themselves of
          what they're missing, I suppose. Paradise Lost. I
          don't know.

WAL: And this one?

FR DESMOND: I bet you don't need telling. I
          bet you're one step ahead of me.

MR BUNTING: Because his wife got ill. He
          didn't have the faith to cope with it. Oh ye of
          little faith! He should've asked the Lord for a
          miracle like I would have done!

WAL: Not just his wife. (WAL
          STRUGGLES TO DIGEST IT). It's a bloody
          jigsaw puzzle, this one!

FR DESMOND: But all the pieces are there, Wal.

WAL: The daughter… the son… he
          lost his faith and then…

MR BUNTING: A miracle! The prodigal
          returned!

WAL: But only his family said so. Witnesses, you said. That's it then. They lied. To get him the comfort... They lied about him coming back.

FR DESMOND: Worse than that. He left a letter saying he was not to be buried in consecrated ground, not to have the last rites, not to give in to the faith of his family! They destroyed the letter.

WAL: Then the daughter...

FR DESMOND: Couldn't live with it. Couldn't live in the church that she'd lied to. And the mother lost her health.

WAL: But the old man kept coming.

FR DESMOND: And never took communion again.

WAL: What happened then?

FR DESMOND: Nothing happened then. The mother died and there was a funeral at the church and the old man came to that along with his daughter and her Protestant husband. But they none of them took communion.

WAL: But that can't be the end of it!

FR DESMOND: No, it can't. But it's the end as far as *I* know. The old man kept coming to church but never partook of the body of Christ. The daughter stayed in her new church.

WAL: So where's the miracle?

FR DESMOND: Doesn't it say something about the moral nature of people that they will lie to their priest and lie to their God to save one of their own, one that's lost his faith? Isn't that tragic, Wal? Isn't that noble in its way? And tormented? And foolish? Isn't it a miracle that people can be so exalted?

WAL: Oh, that's better than mine. (APPROVINGLY) That's wicked, that is.

MR BUNTING: (MISUNDERSTANDING) I agree with *you*, Wal. For once I have got to agree with you. It's wicked, that's what it is. No more, no less. And the wages of sin is death. As the Good Book tells us. Everybody knows that. And that story proves it. *You've* proved it, Father! Because there's hell an' all for them as deserves it an' no mistake! (HE SMACKS HIS KNEE TO EMPHASISE THE REMARK) I've *seen* hell, I've felt its flames. But, thank God, I've come to me senses and believed in Jesus. That's what you should do, Wal, like your friend said, your friend what worked on the buses, before it's too late… (GETS TO HIS FEET, STRIKES POSE) There's always them as mock, of course. Them as come to meetings to mock and jeer. I've had my share of 'em and I've told them to their faces: *the Lord will not be mocked*! *The Lord will find you out*! Oh, and 'e does! He always does! That's one thing you can count on. There was one chap, as I remember, come down to a meeting I used to hold in Cannon Hall Park. Always talking back at me, he was, this Albert summat, his brother lived in Duke Street. Oh and there 'e was, bright as a button, bit of an intellectual so 'e thought, big and strong and healthy, years of life ahead of him, shouting out against the word of the Lord, the worse for strong drink, you could tell. Just wait, I said, the Lord will find you out. Well, one day 'e isn't there, but 'is brother comes round to see me afterwards. *You've got to come and see 'im*, he says, *'e's asked for you.* And it turns out 'e's got some sort of illness, summat the doctors theirselves 'as got no name for. And he's dying, big 'ealthy lookin' fella in the prime of life. *Well*, I says, *I'll go and see 'im, but I've got me calls to make first.* Because I always 'ad me calls to do, sick people and old age pensioners that couldn't never get out, couldn't come to hear the word. But I get round to 'is house later on and he's lying in bed surrounded by 'is cronies, 'is drinking mates, though there's not a drop being taken that day, I can tell you. And they make way for me and I says: *I've come to see you, lad.* And 'e looks at me and 'e says: *I'm gonna die, Mr Bunting.* And I says: *Repent and believe in the Lord, my son, and you shall be saved.* And you know what he says? I'll never forget it till the day I die. *Piss on your Lord!* he says, *and piss on you too!* and he turns away from me. One of 'is mates says: *Don't go, Mr Bunting – you're 'is only hope.* But I says: *I can do no good while 'is heart is hardened against the truth.* Still, I waited on a bit and 'ad a cup of tea and told some of these others about the path to salvation. I was there about 20 minutes when suddenly 'e shouts out from the bed. *Lift me up,* he says. So the others lift 'im up and shake 'is pillow to make 'im more comfortable. *Lift me up*, he says, *lift me up.* So they lift 'im, two round 'is body, one round 'is legs, and they lift 'im and they put 'im down again to make 'im more comfortable. *Lift me up!* he shouts, *Lift me up!* and 'e starts screaming. You never heard such a racket! And they lift 'im up. *Higher! Higher!* he shouts and 'e's screaming away. *Lift me higher!* he shouts, *The flames of 'ell are lickin' me!* And then he dies. (BEAT) Well, if I'd needed any proof of the Lord's ways, I'd've got it allright that day, eh Father? If I needed any proof, which I never did!

THE OTHERS GAZE AT HIM, HORROR-STRUCK. SUDDENLY THERE IS A SCREAM OF ANGUISH FROM OUTSIDE, FOLLOWED BY HYSTERICAL WEEPING. FR DESMOND LEAPS TO HIS FEET, THEN HESITATES. AFTER ABOUT HALF A MINUTE, BILLY RUSHES IN STAGE RIGHT

MR BUNTING: Billy! I've been looking for you for hours. I've had phone calls out to the wards. Where've you been? Chatting up them West Indian nurses on geriatrics again, is it? I thought the charge nurse told you to stay away from there.

BILLY: I been sitting with 'em. Those old people. I been sitting with them. The parents.

FR DESMOND: Those bloody hard chairs! Canvas and steel! Oh, I do my best, Wal, but the flesh is weak.

BILLY : I've been sitting listening. Listening to them tell me about him. But not listening. Not wanting to listen. I've just been there.

FR DESMOND: On those bloody hard chairs. Bloody hard ride. Bloody 250cc. Cut–price offer.

MR BUNTING: (INDIGNANT) We've not got much better in here, Father. Not exactly luxury. Not what you'd call *comfortable* chairs. Though I have requisitioned some from the children's

ward when they close it down in April. I look
after my staff, I do.

FR DESMOND: And hard bloody heart! Weak
arse and hard heart. (TO BILLY) Thanks, Billy.
I better go now. I better do what I can. (EXITS
HURRIEDLY STAGE RIGHT)

MR BUNTING: What was he going on about?
Hard chairs? Them two that I got out of X–ray
are lovely. Nice upright backs to them so you
don't bend in the wrong places. Keep you firm,
they do.

BILLY: I better go. I better go with
Father Desmond. They know me.

MR BUNTING: Well, they'll know *him*. They'll
know who *he* is allright. He's wearing his dog
collar for a start. And he was talkin' to 'em
earlier on. Oh, they'll remember him. Don't
worry about that.

BILLY: I better go. (EXITS STAGE
RIGHT)

MR BUNTING: Well, I'd never buy my son a
motor bike, not 250 cc or 500 cc or whatever
they ride nowadays, not seeing what *I've* seen
over the years, knowing what *I* know, watching
all them accident cases come in here. Not that
I've *got* a son. Nor a daughter neither. Still, I
count that a blessing, I do. I reckon the Almighty
decided I wasn't to have no children. And he
was right. Man who is born of woman… (TONE
BECOMES MORE MATTER–OF–FACT)
Well, it had to happen. We was only waiting for
it. And Father Desmond doesn't have to stay on
half the live-long day now it's over. Over and

done with. They'll be ringing me up any minute now to take the body out of the ward but I reckon I can leave that to the day men. Anyway, I suppose Father Desmond has got some more things to say, a few incantations I wouldn't be surprised, a few Papist things I shouldn't wonder, that I don't really want to be involved in, so we won't disturb. I don't really hold with Papist things. (BEAT) Oh, it's a real cushy number this night work. Easiest shift I ever done in my life. I never knew 'ow cushy it was, Wal. You night men don't know how easy you've got it… And I expect Father Desmond and Billy'll want a cup of tea when they get back. I know *I'd* like another. Come on, Wal. Make us a cup! Chop! Chop! … Oh, I do feel a need to relieve meself though. Make some room for another cup.

HE LAUGHS, EXITS STAGE LEFT IN A RUSH

WAL PICKS UP THE MUGS ONE BY ONE THEN SUDDENLY STAMPS ON ANOTHER WOODLOUSE AND THROWS THE MUGS DOWN IN A HEAP ON HIS CHAIR AT THE BACK. HE GOES OVER TO ONE OF THE CHAIRS STAGE FRONT AND SITS DOWN WEARILY. HE PICKS UP THE COPY OF THE SUN

WAL :   (ANGRILY) Go on! Give me some tit to make me feel better. (WE HEAR FLUSH OF TOILET) Reincarnation! If he ain't careful, 'e'll flush 'isself away. And *he* won't come back as a donkey in a bleedin' straw hat – he'll come back as a fuckin' woodlouse, that one!

LIGHTS DIM
END

All Good Men

...is a comedy of manners about the last days of a once popular Labour government, set in a parallel universe that still manages to resemble Britain. It was premiered in 2010 at The Carriageworks theatre in Leeds, and then went on to the Victoria Hall in Saltaire, as part of a double bill *Sex and Politics*, performed by the Encore Theatre Company. Cast and crew:

Simon Bloom..Lee Petcher
Lorna Bloom...Mia Vore
Darius..Ian Baxter
Ronnie, Lady Bridgewater...............................Carol Plant
Sir Marcus Bridgewater.....................................Alan Brent
Pete Porter...Colin Lewisohn

Directed by Audrey Coldron
Running time: 60 minutes.

Very much of its time, the play was performed only weeks before the General Election that would send Labour back into the wilderness.

Characters

Simon Bloom, a young journalist, middle class, intelligent, attractive, on the make
Ronnie, Lady Bridgewater, 40-something, upper class, beautiful, smart, ruthless, sexy
Darius (pronounced Da-*ry*-us, not *Da*-ree-us), the minister for education, 40-something, upper class, intelligent, sophisticated, witty, attractive, ambitious
Lorna, Simon's wife, young, middle class, pretty, pregnant and fed up

Sir Marcus Bridgewater, Ronnie's husband, health minister, 60-something, upper class, charming but empty

Pete Porter, deputy prime minister, 40-something, portly, working class and proud of it, constantly mangles his sentences

Announcer, voice only, male

Party Conference Chairperson, voice only, female

BBC news reader/announcer, voice only, either sex, any age

Setting: Corridors and hotel rooms at a Labour Party conference in the last days of government.

Time: Very nearly the end of the world.

Furniture: A sofabed, covered with different throws to indicate different beds and sofas in different rooms. Two chairs, to be covered with different throws to indicate different chairs in different rooms. A lectern. A trolley for serving drinks.

Props: A large number of whisky, wine, brandy bottles etc, whisky and wine glasses etc, corkscrews, coasters, wine coolers etc. Two remote control devices, one simple and black, the other complex and silver. An up-to-date copy of the *Economist* magazine. A paperback copy of *Clausewitz on War*. A sheaf of paper to be used as speech notes. Three A1 size election style posters, one each for Jack Peeple, Pete Porter, and Marcus Bridgewater.

STAGE IN DARKNESS. MUSIC: JERUSALEM
SUNG BY A CHOIR. LIGHTS COME UP AT THE
BACK TO REVEAL, STAGE RIGHT, HUGE POSTER
OF HANDSOME, KENNEDY-TYPE MIDDLE-AGED
MAN WITH LEGEND *JACK PEEPLE – MAN OF THE
PEOPLE*. IT IS EDGED IN BLACK. WE HEAR
BACKGROUND HUBBUB OF CONFERENCE
VOICES THEN VOICE OF PARTY CONFERENCE
CHAIRPERSON

CHAIR: (DISEMBODIED VOICE) And now I
        introduce to delegates at this historic party
        conference, our deputy leader and Deputy Prime
        Minister, the Rt Hon Peter Porter MP.

LIGHTS AT BACK DIM. THERE IS POLITE
APPLAUSE AND COUGHING WHICH SUBSIDES
AS PETE ENTERS FROM THE AUDIENCE STAGE
RIGHT UNDER SPOTLIGHT WITH SHEAF OF
PAPERS. HE DROPS A FEW PAPERS, BENDS
OVER, PICKS THEM UP, MOVES NERVOUSLY
ACROSS TO LECTERN, STAGE RIGHT. THE SPOT
FOLLOWS HIM. HE COUGHS, LOOKS ROUND
AND BEGINS HIS ADDRESS

PETE: (ADDRESSING AUDIENCE) Miss or
        Mrs or Ms, as the case may be, Party Conference
        Chairperson, (BEAT) delegates, fellow MPs and
        lady MPs, I address you on this historic and, if I
        may say so, and there is none more apt than I
        myself to make such a comment, such an
        awesome and mournful hour.

SIMON: (DISEMBODIED VOICE) Did he really
        say there is none more apt than I myself?

DARIUS: (DISEMBODIED VOICE) Did he really
        say awesome and mournful hour? (SINGS) *Oh,*

*de mother and child reunion is no more than a
motion away!*

BLUE SPOT TO SIMULATE TV GLARE COMES ON
STAGE CENTRE. DARIUS AND SIMON SIT ON
TWO CHAIRS FACING THE AUDIENCE, DARIUS
ON SIMON'S RIGHT. BOTH HAVE GLASSES IN
THEIR HANDS. ON THE FLOOR ARE A BOTTLE
OF WHISKY, A TELEPHONE AND A SMALL,
BLACK TV REMOTE CONTROL.

PETE: (ADDRESSING AUDIENCE) Jack
Peeple, our great Prime Minister, the wisely and
widely chosen leader of our great party, is
suddenly gone from us. (RAISES HIS HANDS
IN SUPPLICATION) He has suddenly passed
away. As some of you will undoubtedly have
heard already. It was, I believe, in all the
morning papers. Though some of them, of
course, as you know, I never read. (RAISES
VOICE IN ANGER) Because they print nothing
but lies about us. (BEAT) Except that, in this
case, as behoves the death of our leader and
prime minister, Jack Peeple, they are correct.
(BEAT) For once. (BEAT) Even in the midst of
life it seems we are otherwise engaged. (BEAT)
This is a sad day for our party and for anyone
who believes – as we all of us do – in democracy
and the fellowship of the common man!

SPOT GOES OFF STAGE RIGHT. ONLY SIMON
AND DARIUS ARE STILL IN THE LIGHT.
SUDDENLY DARIUS PICKS UP THE REMOTE,
POINTS IT AT THE AUDIENCE AND FLICKS OFF
THE INVISIBLE TV. THE BLUE SPOT GOES OFF.
LIGHTS GO UP CENTRE STAGE ILLUMINATING
SIMON AND DARIUS

DARIUS: No wonder audience figures are plummeting. (HE THROWS THE REMOTE INTO A CORNER)

SIMON: (SLIGHTLY DRUNK) Darius - did Pete, our celebrated deputy prime minister, in this historic TV broadcast, which you have just now consigned to oblivion, really say *as behoves the death of our leader?*

DARIUS: (MORE THAN SLIGHTLY DRUNK) Simon, Simon, correct me if I'm wrong – did he really say *the widely chosen leader of our great party?* Or is it that I've drunk too much of this stuff? (INDICATES GLASS)

SIMON: No, he really said it. Though, to be fair, you *have* drunk too much Johnny Walker. *Far* too much. That's what you always do when you come to the party conference and there's a free drinks cabinet in the hotel room. (BEAT) And did Pete really say *in the midst of life we are otherwise engaged*? Did he really say *the fellowship of the common man*?

DARIUS: Fellowship? He's been reading *The Lord of the Rings*. No, he hasn't. Stupid me. He's seen the film. (BEAT) Simon, old son, did he really use the word *democracy*? That's the really difficult part to believe.

SIMON: He must have been reading *The New Statesman*. No, no. Who am I kidding? There's probably a video game called *Grand Theft Democracy*. (PUTS GLASS DOWN ON FLOOR, COUNTS ON HIS FINGERS) *De-moc-ra-cy*. That's four syllables at one go! He must be having elocution lessons.

DARIUS: Well, enough of situation comedy.
           Uncle Jack's gone at last, surprise victim of the
           Big C. Cancer strikes where voters fear to tread.

SIMON: Some of your gremlins on the Left were
           saying he was losing popularity anyway.

DARIUS: But he still produced a working majority
           of 68. Which was at least 69 more than his last
           three predecessors. (BEAT) Now everything's
           up for grabs. Place your bets, gentlemen. Roll
           up, roll up! The leadership of the party is today's
           glittering prize.

SIMON: Darius, let me ask, give me a straight
           answer for once: are you throwing your cap into
           the ring?

DARIUS: Caps! Caps are for people like Pete, the
           man in the street, the oik on the clapped-out
           omnibus. Not for the likes of thee and me.
           (BEAT) But no, Simon. I'm not ready. I'm still
           minister of Education, don't forget. The bed of
           nails. Of course, we should be expelling the
           knife carriers and the drug dealers from our
           schools. But if we do that, we're not inclusive
           any more.

SIMON: So you're making do with metal
           detectors, barbed wire and sniffer dogs.

DARIUS: As you said yourself, in that excellent
           speech you wrote for me, we can't endlessly
           protect our pupils from the rigours of the adult
           environment. We have to prepare them for Class
           A drugs and sudden death in a dark alley.

SIMON: That doesn't sound like me. Not sudden death in a dark alley. No, I'm fairly sure I never said that.

DARIUS: Well, you said it better than that. But that's what you meant. You know you did. And as for the exam system, which you chose not to mention, your average Golden Retriever could get three Grade As with a star these days. (BEAT) In fact, some already have. But we're forcing the Kennel Club to stay quiet about it.

SIMON: So what's on the cards for you following this deadly turn of events?

DARIUS: Give me another two years, and I might get an invisible ministry. You know, something that doesn't need any results at all. Something like Environment where I can go on about carbon footprints and bollock the Japanese for killing too many whales. At least we're never going to be inclusive about the Japanese. (BEAT) You know, I never thought the Grim Reaper would force Old Jack to make a quick exit. Nobody did.

SIMON: So. Who's going to be the next Prime Minister?

DARIUS: Well, I'll tell you who *won't* get it. It won't be Pete , the Last of the Working Class. The man who thinks angina is the female sex organ. Our exalted deputy leader was only chosen for that purely nominal position to help us keep the imbecile vote. A symbol of our time, that's Pete, the Acceptable Face of the Political Sweepstake – proof positive that *anyone* can make it if he's lucky and keeps hanging about for long enough.

SIMON: So?

DARIUS: So there are different rules for the top job. (BEAT) I know, let's make a list of candidates. Everybody will be doing it anyway.

SIMON: I haven't got a pen.

DARIUS: You don't need one. (BEAT) Right. Let's look at the women, for a start.

SIMON: Always worth doing. Looking at women.

DARIUS: Absolutely. Never forget the women. All of them dreaming their wet Maggie Thatcher dreams. Peeple's Poppets, as the Sun is always calling them.

SIMON: Except…

DARIUS: Except they haven't got what it takes. None of them.

SIMON: Not Donna Sands? Not even Gemma Hanley?

DARIUS: If Gemma Hanley had two more brain cells, she'd be a plant. And the Sands woman has a very fat arse. Donna Kebab, as the Currant Bun likes to call her. (BEAT) OK. We've done the women. What about the men?

SIMON: Nobody springing easily to mind. Not to *my* mind anyway. Not since Harry Crane got stopped for drink driving.

DARIUS: A home secretary who's just delayed the police service annual pay rise for three months ought to know better than to get pissed and fall asleep behind the wheel. (BEAT) And Jerry Stevens ought to know better than to sleep with his secretary.

SIMON: Especially when his secretary is an ex-commando. He was actually a sergeant major, wasn't he? Special Operations Group.

THEY BOTH BURST OUT LAUGHING. AFTER A FEW SECONDS THE PHONE RINGS. DARIUS LEANS ACROSS TO PICK UP THE RECEIVER

DARIUS: (INTO PHONE) OK, Marcus. Yes, he's here right now, as a matter of fact. (BEAT) Well, I'll tell him of your interest. Yes, I'm sure he'll be flattered. (BEAT) OK, Marcus. Love to Ronnie. (BEAT) OK.

HE HANGS UP AND TURNS TO SIMON

DARIUS: Well, well. Marcus Bridgewater is in need of your services, you silver-tongued arsehole. Our beleaguered health minister, whose very own hospitals probably did more to dispatch Old Jack than the whole tobacco industry, wants you to work on one of his speeches. And he asked me if you were available. Now, he's one name we *didn't* pull out of the hat. Silly us. I think he'll probably want to go for Jack's job, the old bugger. And he just might get it.

SIMON: Because there's nobody else?

DARIUS: Because he's been around a long time and never done anything stupid. Not *very* stupid anyway. Actually, he's never done anything, full stop. That's why people think he's a safe pair of hands.

SIMON: Why'd he ask *you*? Why didn't he come to me direct?

DARIUS: He must think I'm your manager. Anyway, he's in his suite on the 22nd floor, only 15 floors above us, eagerly awaiting your visit. (BEAT) I told you – you're a star round here. Ever since you wrote that speech for me, you know (BEAT) the one that defied the conventional wisdom of the Polly Toynbees of this world by supporting larger classrooms. When you suggested that having more than 40 in a class wasn't just a damn sight cheaper but was actually a better way to deliver vocational training to adolescent black boys, it made a lot of people think. Especially in the Treasury. (BEAT) Well, don't just sit there. (WAVES HIS HAND) Go on. Pop along. Might do you some good. Might do us both some good.

SIMON: (PUTTING DOWN HIS GLASS) I'll have to brush my teeth first. (BEAT) And I'd better pop in and see Lorna. That's (BEAT) only three floors down.

DARIUS: That's right. Splash on some water. Sober up. Impress old Marcus. He can do more for you than *I* ever could. (BEAT) Well, he can if he gets the job.

LIGHTS GO DOWN STAGE CENTRE. LIGHTS COME UP STAGE LEFT REVEALING SMALL BED. LYING ACROSS IT, FULLY CLOTHED, IS LORNA, READING *THE ECONOMIST*. THERE IS SOUND OF KEY IN LOCK. LORNA LOOKS ACROSS AS

SIMON ENTERS STAGE LEFT WITH KEY IN
HAND.

SIMON:　　　Sweetheart. Lover. Beloved wife. Love
　　　　　　of my Life. Mmmmmmmm. (BLOWS KISS)

LORNA:　　　(LOOKING UP) You've been drinking.

SIMON:　　　Just because I'm paying you
　　　　　　compliments, you think I've been drinking?
　　　　　　Hah! (BEAT) Got to rush. Dying for a piss.

HE EXITS LIGHTED AREA STAGE RIGHT. WE
HEAR SOUND OF BATHROOM DOOR, TOILET LID
RAISED, PISSING, FLUSHING, BATHROOM DOOR
AGAIN

SIMON:　　　(RE-ENTERING LIGHTED AREA)
　　　　　　You should have come with me to see Darius.
　　　　　　You know he thinks the world of you.

LORNA:　　　(REMAINS LYING ON BED,
　　　　　　RETURNS TO READING) No, Simon. *You're*
　　　　　　the one he thinks the world of. His brilliant
　　　　　　speech writer! And, of course, there's always
　　　　　　Darius himself. We mustn't forget that. Darius
　　　　　　thinks the world of Darius too.

SIMON:　　　He's a politician. They're all the same.
　　　　　　(BEAT) Where's the spare head for the electric
　　　　　　toothbrush?

LORNA:　　　(WITHOUT LOOKING UP) I don't
　　　　　　know. Use the one *I* used. It's not as if you're
　　　　　　going to catch anything from me. I'm the one
　　　　　　who catches things from you.

SIMON DISAPPEARS STAGE RIGHT ONCE MORE.
SOUNDS OF ELECTRIC TOOTHBRUSH. LORNA IS

STILL SILENTLY TURNING PAGES. FINALLY
SIMON RE-ENTERS LIGHTED AREA, RUSHES
FORWARD AND KISSES HER BRIEFLY

SIMON: (SITTING ON BED NEXT TO
               LORNA) You used to like the conference
               season. The sea air. The *hot* air. You used to
               enjoy all the gossip and the plotting. (BEAT)
               And you had political ambitions yourself. When
               we first met. When we were both reporters.

LORNA: (SHE FINALLY LOOKS UP) Now I'm
               just your wife.

SIMON: (JOSHING HER) Oh, come on! You're
               the best deputy chief sub in the business. What
               would *Woman's Own* do without you?

LORNA: Now I'm just your *pregnant* wife.

SIMON: (AMAZED) You're kidding!
               (GRAPPLES BRIEFLY WITH THE
               CONCEPT) Oh my God! That's (BEAT)
               wonderful!

HE FALLS ON BED, HUGS HER AND SMOTHERS
HER FACE IN KISSES. SHE REMAINS
UNIMPRESSED

LORNA: I'm glad you think so. I'm glad the man
               of the household is pleased.

SIMON: You're absolutely sure? I mean, when
               did you know for certain? Did you see one of the
               local quacks down here?

LORNA: God, you're so old fashioned! You don't
               need a doctor these days, Simon. A woman

doesn't need a doctor to tell her when she's up the spout. (BEAT) I've known a few days.

SIMON: (TAKEN ABACK) Well (BEAT) well, it's great! (GETTING UP OFF THE BED) You don't have to give up your job, you know. You don't have to take on the whole mother thing yourself. We might be able to afford a nanny. In fact, I'm sure we will. Even with the credit crunch. Get a nice Rumanian girl or something. I could be on my way to greater things, you know. Real success. People think a lot of me here.

LORNA: (RETURNING TO HER READING) The party people.

SIMON: Yes. (BEAT) Well, there seem to be a few new openings all of a sudden. Give me a little time and *I* might be the one who gives up being a hack. (BEAT) And that's where I'm going now. To see someone. Sir Marcus Bridgewater, no less. Cabinet minister. Maybe prime minister in the not so distant. (BEAT) That's what I meant about affording a nanny.

LORNA: (NOT LOOKING UP) So you've got to rush off?

SIMON: But I won't be long. *Would* I be long? Would I be *long*? (BEAT) Oh, it's great. Can I tell people? I want to, I really do. Can I tell them about the baby?

LORNA: (LOOKING UP BRIEFLY) Sure. It'll save me the job. (SHE GOES BACK TO HER MAGAZINE)

SIMON: (LEAPING TO HIS FEET) Yes. Yes, it will. You rest. Take it easy. Right. OK.

HE EXITS LIGHTED AREA STAGE LEFT. SOUND
OF DOOR SLAMMING. LIGHTS GO DOWN STAGE
LEFT. LIGHTS COME UP STAGE RIGHT FRONT
REVEALING LARGE SOFA, WHERE RONNIE,
WEARING A BATH TOWEL, LIES ON HER
STOMACH, READING A PAPERBACK. SUDDENLY
THERE IS A LOUD BUZZING NOISE. RONNIE
REACHES OVER TO A LARGE AND COMPLEX
SILVER REMOTE CONTROL DEVICE, PICKS IT UP

RONNIE: (SPEAKING INTO REMOTE) Hello.
      Who's there?

SIMON: (DISEMBODIED VOICE,
      DISTORTED SLIGHTLY) It's Simon Bloom. Is
      Sir Marcus Bridgewater there?

RONNIE PRESSES SWITCH ON REMOTE AND WE
HEAR MECHANICAL SOUND OF DOOR OPENING
THEN CLOSING. RONNIE GETS UP FROM SOFA,
SMOOTHING HER FRONT. ENTER SIMON, STAGE
RIGHT

SIMON: (TAKEN ABACK) Oh, I'm sorry. I
      didn't realise…

RONNIE: Realise?

SIMON: That you were…

RONNIE: I was just thinking of taking a shower.

SIMON: I'm sorry. I'll come back.

RONNIE: I don't see why. You don't have to take
      a shower *with* me. Unless you're *really* dirty.

SIMON: But if it's inconvenient…

RONNIE: I can put it off. (LAUGHS) The shower, I mean, not the towel. (BEAT) God, you're very shy. That must be what comes from going to a state school. (BEAT) Look, don't worry. I *am* wearing knickers. Honest. (SHE OPENS THE FRONT OF HER TOWEL TO SHOW HIM HER KNICKERS) See. And the top part isn't going to fall down. I have all the necessary superstructure. Flying buttresses, Marcus calls them.

SIMON: Yes, I'm sure he does.

RONNIE: Simon Bloom. (BEAT) Are you a Jew?

SIMON: (TAKEN BY SURPRISE) No. (BEAT) Not that…

RONNIE: Not that it matters. Don't worry. Marcus's mother was a Jew.

SIMON: But, as it happens, *I'm* not. It's not a thing I'd ever deny. If it were true. I'd be proud of it. But I just don't happen to *be* a Jew. That's why I said no. That's the only reason. (BEAT) Actually, my parents were Methodists.

RONNIE: Ah, a proud young Methodist! (BEAT) Of course. Nobody's suggesting anything different.

SIMON: (GETS HOLD OF HIMSELF) Is Sir Marcus… ?

RONNIE: You can just call him Marcus. When he gets here. And I'll just call you Simon.

SIMON: I was told Sir Marcus was here.

RONNIE: He's not. But *I* am.

SIMON: You're *Mrs* Bridgewater?

RONNIE: *Lady* Bridgewater. But well done anyway. You can call me Ronnie.

SIMON: Is that short for Veronica?

RONNIE: No.

SIMON: (EVENTUALLY RECOVERING HIS COMPOSURE) What were you reading?

RONNIE: *Clausewitz on War.*

SIMON: Oh, right. *War is diplomacy by other means.*

RONNIE: But I have a theory of my own. (BEAT) *Diplomacy is war by other means.* (BEAT) You're allowed to laugh. Unless, of course, you didn't find it funny.

SIMON: (WITH FORCED LAUGH) Oh yes, I did. I *did*. (BEAT) Where is... Marcus?

RONNIE: To tell you the truth, I'm not at all sure. I hope he's not dead. Not after what happened to Jack. Two deaths at one party conference would just confuse the press. And who knows – they might start looking for suspects. (BEAT) Oh, I forgot. You *are* the press. Some of the time. *The Independent*, isn't it? Subeditor or something. Aren't you?

SIMON: Yes. I am. Well, most of the time.

RONNIE: That's confusing. You'll have to make up your mind pretty soon. Which way to jump. The Montagues or the Capulets. (BEAT) Do you want a drink?

SIMON: Yes. Yes, please. That would be very nice.

RONNIE: Whisky, vodka?

SIMON: (CATCHING HIMSELF) Oh no. Bit early for the hard stuff. (BEAT) White wine. If you've got it.

RONNIE: (SHE SHOOTS HIM A LOOK) Of course we've got it. Chardonnay. Sauvignon. Chenin Blanc. (BEAT) Floor 22. We're practically a wine cellar in the sky. (BEAT) I'll take a look in the kitchen.

SHE LEAVES THE LIGHTED AREA STAGE LEFT. SIMON WALKS SLOWLY ROUND, PATS THE CUSHIONS ON THE SOFA, PICKS UP THE REMOTE CONTROL AND BRIEFLY PLAYS WITH IT UNTIL IT MAKES A BUZZING SOUND.HE PRESSES A BUTTON AND THE VOICE OF AN ANNOUNCER COMES ON THE INVISIBLE TV.

ANNOUNCER: Although property prices were down last month…

SIMON DROPS THE REMOTE IN SURPRISE AND STARTS BACK. THE TV SOUND STOPS SUDDENLY

RONNIE: (DISEMBODIED VOICE) Would you like me to suck your cock?

SIMON: (STARTLED) What?

RONNIE: (ENTERING LIGHTED AREA
            PUSHING A TROLLEY WITH BOTTLES
            AND GLASSES) I said: would you like
            Chardonnay or Hock?

SIMON: (RECOVERS) Chardonnay will do.

RONNIE: Yes. That's what I think of Chardonnay.
            It will always do. (SHE UNSCREWS CAP ON
            THE BOTTLE) I like a screw. Rather than a
            cork, I mean. (BEAT) I just won't waste what's
            left of my life on synthetic corks any more.
            (SHE HANDS SIMON A GLASS)

SIMON: (TAKING THE GLASS) I suppose
            that's one way of looking at it.

RONNIE: There are lots of ways of looking at it.
            There are lots of ways of looking at most things.
            But you're a journalist. You'd know that.
            What's your perception of the National Health
            Service for instance?

SIMON: Well...

RONNIE: (INTERRUPTING) Because it's
            something Marcus is very much concerned
            about. Being health minister. (BEAT) We've
            probably got as good a health service as any
            developed country. Except for France. And
            Spain. And possibly Germany and the
            Netherlands. And we have to keep watching
            America. And certainly things are improving in
            Poland these days. But Marcus is such a
            traditionalist. He sees himself as the keeper of
            the flame. (BEAT) That's only a metaphor of
            course. But I can talk about metaphors to an
            educated young man like you, can't I? You may

be a headline writer but you're not embarrassed by big words.

SIMON: Oh no.

RONNIE: Tell me about your university. It was Balliol, wasn't it?

SIMON: Yes.

RONNIE: Darius says you're a wizard with words. You were up with Darius's brother, weren't you?

SIMON: Young Jamie. Yes. We're good friends. That's how I met Darius.

RONNIE: And you're a scholarship boy. Didn't even go to public school. I admire that. (BEAT) Don't worry. Nobody would guess it from the way you talk.

SIMON: How *do* I talk?

RONNIE: With such confidence. (BEAT) Confidence is what government is all about, don't you agree?

SIMON: Yes. I suppose.

RONNIE: No suppose about it. No suppose allowed. Confidence in our institutions. (BEAT) How would you feel if you couldn't find a dentist? Lots of people say they can't find one these days. How would you perceive it? If no dentist would take you on because it wasn't worth his while any more? (BEAT) And don't think I'm being sexist saying *he*. Most dentists *are* men, aren't they? Poking about in your openings is something a man is naturally better at doing. (BEAT) How would you feel?

SIMON: (THINKS ABOUT IT) Feel? Let me think. I'd feel it was up to me to keep my teeth healthy.

RONNIE: Go on.

SIMON: Self reliance is a British virtue.

RONNIE: Yes. Yes. I like that.

SIMON: (WARMING TO HIS THEME) Nobody likes sitting in a dentist's chair, anyway… Having someone...

RONNIE: … poke about in your openings..

SIMON: I'd think prevention is better than cure. If I had the…

RONNIE: Drop-in centre…

SIMON: Where I could go to be…

RONNIE: Reassured.

SIMON: Reassured.

RONNIE: A nurse with one of those little mirror things and mouthwash in a plastic cup. (BEAT) Well, I say a *nurse*. Some girl in a white coat wearing her name on her breast.

SIMON: Do away with the dentist.

RONNIE: No more pain, embarrassment, poking about. (BEAT) Give me a slogan. For Marcus's speech.

SIMON: Be-sharper-with-your-teeth. Make-your-mouth-matter.

RONNIE: Yes. That's good. In fact, that's worth a telly ad. I mean, an information campaign to let people know what's happening in their health service. (BEAT) Aren't you writing this down?

SIMON: I didn't bring a notebook.

RONNIE: Then I suppose I'll just have to remember it all. Luckily, I do have total recall. (BEAT) Alright. Let's change the subject. Superbugs. Oh, I do hate that word. It's very unscientific. (BEAT) A lot of people these days are pathetically afraid of them. They think every time they go into hospital for an in-growing toenail, they're risking their lives. And it's just not true. A lot of infected people recover. Up to a point.

SIMON: It's the patient's fault.

RONNIE: How?

SIMON: (THINKS ABOUT IT) They bring the bugs in with them. Or their visitors do.

RONNIE: You can't stop visitors.

SIMON: (WARMING TO IT) Wait. It's like wartime. Appeal to their better nature.

RONNIE: Go on.

SIMON: My mum says her mum said they used to have a slogan in the war. *Is your journey really necessary?* Well, how about: Is your *visit* really necessary? No, there's got to be a better way of saying it. Something alliterative. (BEAT) *Don't wear out your welcome on the wards.*

RONNIE: That's good. You can almost sing it.

SIMON: So again you're appealing to people's sense of responsibility. Making them responsible. In a way, you're empowering them.

RONNIE: I like it. But I wonder if it's going far enough? (BEAT) If we actually succeed in cutting back on hospital visits and the bugs are still... well, bugging, it won't look good. (BEAT) Let me put it bluntly. It's the patients we're really aiming at.

SIMON: Er... I haven't really thought it through, have I?

RONNIE: Never mind. We'll get there in the end. Say it anyway. We're only brainstorming here. (BEAT) There's nobody else in the room.

SIMON: OK. It's the same idea we had with the dentist. (BEAT) No-one wants to go into hospital. If you do go, it tells the whole world there's something badly wrong with you...

RONNIE: You're sick... unhealthy. Nobody wants that.

SIMON: You've been doing something wrong. Not looking after yourself. Smoking. Drinking too much. (HE SUDDENLY BECOMES AWARE OF THE GLASS IN HIS HAND AND

PUTS IT DOWN ON THE TROLLEY.
RONNIE POURS HIM ANOTHER)

RONNIE: So hospital's the last resort?

SIMON: Exactly. An admission of failure.

RONNIE: What's the alternative? Gyms. Health
            clubs. Exercise. Keep your weight down. Look
            good. That's the key. That's the positive side.
            And it's a big industry looking to expand. We
            can encourage the change-over. More jobs. Less
            training. No five-year degree courses in
            medicine. And...

SIMON: Vouchers.

RONNIE: *Government* vouchers.

SIMON: Stay healthy. Stay out of hospital. Take
            your voucher along to...

RONNIE: The Lifetime Fitness Centre. Regular
            tests. Blood pressure. Eyesight. AIDS.
            Swimming pool. Exercise bikes. Have your teeth
            whitened.

SIMON: Mind you, there'll be some cost, a lot of
            initial outlay. I mean, if you're putting up drop-
            in clinics all over the place...

RONNIE: Libraries.

SIMON: Libraries?

RONNIE: Oh, I don't mean *real* libraries. I don't
            mean the British Library or university libraries
            or anywhere useful. I mean *public* libraries.
            That's where we'll do it. The Lifetime Fitness

Centre visits your local library three times a week.

SIMON: What about the librarians?

RONNIE: They'll be falling over themselves, believe me. They're always looking for something to do. The middle classes, who used to be able to read, don't go into libraries any more. It's just tramps dossing, noisy kids pretending to do their homework, immigrants looking for porn on the computers. No, no, librarians will love every minute. It'll give them job security. (BEAT) Now. GPs.

SIMON: GPs.

RONNIE: Yes. Nobody likes them. They only spare you five minutes and then they give you a prescription that does you no good at all and it costs the earth.

SIMON: Trust your chemist.

RONNIE: What?

SIMON: Your chemist. (BEAT) He's a shopkeeper. The only small shopkeeper you've got left. You get on with him. He always asks you how your kids are doing at school. It's more than your doctor ever does. He's friendly. He doesn't act superior, like he's got a degree. That's because anyone who actually serves you probably *hasn't* got a degree. Asking your chemist is like asking your neighbour. You know you can trust him. You go to see him anyway when you've got your prescription. This way, you cut out the doctor, cut out the middle-man. Let the chemist write the prescription.

57

RONNIE: It's good. The whole package. Looking after your teeth. Taking responsibility for not spreading germs. Negotiating with your chemist over the medicines you need. Not hanging around surgeries half your life. It's empowerment. Sort of. What do we call it? Come on. You said yourself you need alliteration if you want to get the message across.

SIMON: Ok. Ok (BEAT) *Whole health.* (BEAT) Save time, save energy. Whole health. It shouldn't leave a *hole* in your life.

SILENCE. SIMON AND RONNIE LOOK AT EACH OTHER, RAPT. THEN RONNIE CLUNKS SIMON'S GLASS.

SIMON: So. Did I pass the audition?

RONNIE: Well, there's a lot more to talk about. (BEAT) But I think we've done enough for one day. (BEAT) And I haven't offered my congratulations. (BEAT) I mean, the baby.

SIMON: How did… ?

RONNIE: You're a journalist. You have your sources. So do I. Right now you're feeling very excited about it.

SIMON: Absolutely.

RONNIE: That'll soon pass. The sleepless nights. The stink of fetid nappies. And your wife…

SIMON: Lorna.

RONNIE: She's redbrick, isn't she? Well, I
           suppose she'll want to stay at work, so that'll
           mean a nanny. So. Time for a career change
           anyway.

SIMON: A nanny. Yes. That's what I was
           saying…

RONNIE: And she won't want sex as often as she
           used to. Not when she's been through the result.
           (BEAT) I always find the conference is a hell of
           a turn-on. I bet *she* does too. Usually. All that
           testosterone. You can smell it.

SIMON: Well…

RONNIE: It actually stinks the place out. God,
           even Pete looks half fanciable when he's
           banging his fist on somebody's podium.

SIMON: I don't know about…

RONNIE: She's changed, hasn't she? Suddenly.
           She's started lying on the bed reading library
           books…

SIMON: Magazines. (BEAT) Not silly
           magazines. Political stuff. *The Economist.*

RONNIE: But just flicking through, turning the
           pages, skim-reading…

SIMON: Well…

RONNIE: No conversation. No sly innuendo. No
           toes under the table. No interest in the lower
           things of life. No touching at all in the course of
           your average day. (BEAT) That's why it wasn't
           a surprise to you when she told you. Not really.

You'd suspected for a week or two. So you had to pretend. *What fabulous news, darling!* (BEAT) I bet you do a lot of pretending, Simon. Am I right? (BEAT) I remember how *I* felt when I was having Declan and Roberta. Spent the daylight hours watching Kilroy on the box. Now, of course, I don't have any such distractions. (BEAT) I don't want to come on like Mrs Robinson, Simon. Don't make me spell it out.

SIMON: Your husband…

RONNIE: Call him Marcus. That's what I told you to do.

SIMON: What would he… ?

RONNIE: Say?

SIMON: Do?

RONNIE: Just smile in that certain way of his. Almost charming. (BEAT) He doesn't mind, Ok? It's a relief to him. He's gay. Didn't you know?

SIMON: (GENUINELY SURPRISED) For God's sake! He's never…

RONNIE: …come on to you? Well, that's not surprising. He's never looked the part, thank God. He's never been tempted to have a Mohican haircut.

SIMON: I can't believe…

RONNIE: Why not?

SIMON: But you've got two children. You just said…

RONNIE: Oscar Wilde had a couple of kids.

SIMON: (SHOCKED) You're serious!

RONNIE: I'm never anything else. Just because it's a game doesn't mean you can afford to be flippant.

SIMON: Right.

RONNIE: So we have an understanding then. You and I. And Marcus. So you'll write Marcus's speeches and help him become the next party leader. And your wife will get her nanny. That's social justice for you. Instant karma. (BEAT) Right. (SHE PUTS HER GLASS ON THE TROLLEY)

RONNIE: I hope you don't expect me to undress you. I've never had a Methodist before.

LIGHTS GO DOWN.

TV ANNOUNCER: (DISEMBODIED VOICE) All eyes today will be on the performances of deputy leader Peter Porter and health minister Marcus Bridgewater. Both are being spoken of as potential leaders but neither has officially declared his candidacy and much depends on their state-of-play speeches, defending their records, outlining the successes of the past rather than their plans for the future.

SINGLE SPOT PLAYS ON POSTER OF PETE AT BACK OF STAGE. PETE WALKS FROM THE AUDIENCE STAGE RIGHT INTO ANOTHER SPOT

WHICH FOLLOWS HIM. AGAIN HE IS CARRYING
PAPERS BUT THIS TIME THEY ARE HELD
TOGETHER BY GIANT PAPER CLIP. HE STOPS AT
LECTERN STAGE RIGHT AND BEGINS HIS
SPEECH.

PETE :   (TO AUDIENCE) It has indeed been a
momentous week for our party. Perhaps the most
momentous in recent memory. *Memento Mori,*
as the poets say. So I am told. (BEAT) It's true I
don't read a lot of poetry. As you know. I seem
to be far too busy with the decisions of
government, with deciding on decisions that
have to be made decisively. And it has been a
momentous memento mori from a momentous
leader whom we all realise was irreplaceable. If
you like to think of it that way. Which I do. But
it *is* time to think about replacing him. Even so.
Even though replacing the irreplaceable is
(BEAT) difficult. (BEAT) We began our historic
conference on Monday morning facing the
shocking news of Jack Peeple's sudden demise.
Our historical conference was not however an
hysterical conference. (RAISES VOICE) Not
even our worst enemies, and we know who they
are, could say such a thing of us. (BEAT) The
tears of history, the tears of a nation, were
raining down on us. (BEAT) But we reined in
our feelings and set about the tasks of
government as usual, carrying on and carrying
out the tasks that our leader left for us to take up
and carry on with. We were left in mourning. On
Monday morning we mourned. Mourning came
to us on Monday. (BEAT) But now it is time to
overcome our grief. Now it is time to consign
our grief to the infinite past and pass beyond our
mourning of the leader who passed away.

EXIT PETE STAGE RIGHT. HIS SPOT GOES OFF.

DARIUS: (DISEMBODIED VOICE) You wouldn't think he could get any worse than last time.

SIMON: (DISEMBODIED VOICE) But he has. This only goes to prove what I'm always saying: there *is* a God! (BEAT) One thing that bothers me, Darius...

DARIUS: (DISEMBODIED VOICE) Yes?

SIMON: (DISEMBODIED VOICE) It looks like it's going to be a two-horse race. I don't get it. I thought there'd be half a dozen, just for the hell of it. But it's just Pete and Marcus. As far as I know.

DARIUS: (DISEMBODIED VOICE) Let's hope our man is a bit more impressive then.

SPOT SWITCHES FROM POSTER OF PETE TO POSTER OF MARCUS. ENTER MARCUS, ALSO FROM AUDIENCE INTO ANOTHER SPOTLIGHT, STAGE LEFT. FOLLOWED BY SPOT, HE CROSSES STAGE RIGHT THE LECTERN. HE TOO IS CARRYING SHEAF OF PAPERS. HE STANDS AT LECTERN. WE HEAR POLITE APPLAUSE

MARCUS: (ADDRESSING THE AUDIENCE) You all know me. Marcus Bridgewater. And you all know my passion – good health. But I am here today to tell you to forget about wonder drugs and cutting waiting lists. Any successful health service must first of all take into account its greatest asset – the people of this nation. The patients. (BEAT) Now. Empowerment. What do I mean by that, by what John Lennon once termed *power to the people*? I mean a new sense

of responsibility. (BEAT) I call it Whole
Health because health is a matter of considering
the whole man. Or woman. It means trusting in
the innate wisdom of the man – or woman – in
the street. Prescription advice from the man in
the shop, the man – or woman – who knows.
The man or woman who knows *you*. The man or
woman who talks *your* language, the familiar
language of your own aunt or uncle whose idea
of drawing wisdom from life does not mean
simply drawing a graph on a chart. (BEAT)
Teeth. They do take a large bite out of our
budget. (POLITE LAUGHTER FROM
AUDIENCE) And that is why we must
emphasise the preventive action of the intelligent
patient rather than the gross invasion of our
mouths. Let us give some dignity back to the
dental patient. Let him or her be made more
responsible for what goes on in his – or her –
mouth. Fluoride in our water. A free toothbrush
for all our school students. (BEAT) Now we turn
to sensible action on hospital infections. A visa
system for visitors. (BEAT) You know, I believe
the best cure for sickness is to get back as soon
as possible into the world outside, the world of
health, away from the hospital with its expensive
regime. That's why we will be issuing vouchers
for people who stay out of hospital. (BEAT)
And finally fitness. The Fitness Checklist will be
issued to every adult. (BEAT) Our policy is to
outlaw illness once and for all.

MARCUS EXITS STAGE RIGHT AS HIS
SPOTLIGHT GOES OFF. SPOT ON POSTER OFF.
POLITE APPLAUSE. LIGHTS GO UP STAGE
RIGHT. DARIUS'S HOTEL ROOM AS BEFORE.
SIMON SITS ON ONE OF THE CHAIRS WHILE
RONNIE, NOW DRESSED IN A SMART TROUSER

SUIT, AND DARIUS PACE IN FRONT OF HIM. ALL
THREE HOLD GLASSES

DARIUS: Alright, alright. Phase One is AOK.
                 Marcus has done us proud.

RONNIE: He's re-established himself. I always
                knew he would. Safe pair of hands. Good to
                have around in a crisis. It would be a brave man
                who would attack his record on health matters
                now. He's shown he's got real vision. OK,
                maybe the day-to-day stuff doesn't always work
                out, but he's got good reasons for everything he
                does. He's shown that.

DARIUS: An overview. The big picture. That's
                 what we need more than anything. That's what
                 Marcus has shown he's got.

RONNIE: He may not be a shooting star but he's
                very firm in the long-term.

DARIUS: As you of course are in the best position
                 to verify.

RONNIE: Of course.

DARIUS: And who needs a shooting star anyway?
                 They just fall to earth. And lie there in the wet
                 grass. Like Roman candles on November the
                 sixth.

RONNIE: Right. And, thanks to Simon, people
                have started to appreciate the fact. They've
                started to appreciate Marcus. We've started
                spreading the message.

SIMON: Well, I'm pleased you think so. I like to
                 think I've played my part.

DARIUS: Oh, you have, Simon. Lovely stuff. Beautiful phrasing. Music to the ears of the jaded delegates facing their first real crisis in ten years. That's the trouble. Jack Peeple gave them vision, rhetoric, reassurance, full employment. And when I say full employment, I'm mainly talking about the MPs themselves. Now we've got...

RONNIE: Credit crunch. Property prices falling fast. Jobs jettisoned. Companies crashing. There. You always like alliteration, Simon. Well, we've got all the alliteration you could ask for. But it's all on the wrong side.

DARIUS: We can put that right. We've got the words. Simon's words. *Simon* can put that right.

SIMON: I don't know. Words only go so far. I mean, OK, I can put the best gloss on things. But what's really needed is action. Isn't that right?

DARIUS: Action? Action? I've been in politics over 20 years and that's the most subversive thing I've ever heard. What good do you think action ever does?

SIMON: (PERPLEXED) Well, I...

DARIUS: The second world war. That was action. And Churchill actually won it. Actually bloody won it for us. Against all the odds. What happened to him then?

RONNIE: He lost the election.

SIMON: Yes, but...

DARIUS: Mikhail Gorbachev. Champion of Russian democracy. Survived the coup. Supported free elections. What happened?

RONNIE: Fucking Boris Yeltsin, that's what happened.

DARIUS: George Bush. Senior. Goes to war with Saddam Hussein. BEATs him hollow.

RONNIE: Starts a family tradition.

DARIUS: What happens then?

RONNIE: Bill Clinton.

SIMON: But…

DARIUS: No, my young Simon, my unworldly political person, real action is the last thing any politician should get involved in. Why? Because it defines you. Why is that bad? Because once you are defined, once you show yourself in sharp outline, once your profile is prominent, once you stick your head above the parapet, and all those other bloody clichés, some people discover they actually disagree with you. They may even go so far as to dislike you. Intensely. So they vote for somebody else. (BEAT) So no. No action. (BEAT) It's plans. That's what we need. Vast, huge, open-ended plans that never actually produce a result, because a result is something some people might not like. As long as people can see you're talking about doing something, they assume you *are* doing something. But they're never quite sure what. And that's good. As long as you stick to the words thing, you can always change your mind. If the wind starts blowing in the opposite direction, you can always change tack. You've still got room to manoeuvre.

SIMON: I don't see…

RONNIE: Look. Suppose you're Chancellor of the Exchequer and violent crime is on the increase? The prisons are so overcrowded, they're having to release muggers and rapists after the first weekend. But you haven't built a new prison in ten years because you'd rather spend the money creating new jobs like outreach counsellor for disabled lesbians? What do you do?

SIMON: Well…

DARIUS: You say: *I want to start a national debate on whether we should be sending so many people to prison.* You say: *here I am, asking the electorate to decide for themselves.* How long does the debate go on?

RONNIE: How long is a piece of knicker elastic? Especially when you're eating tons of chocolate?

DARIUS: So no new prisons get built.

RONNIE: But we've got ourselves a faithful army of very satisfied outreach workers. Who always vote for us.

DARIUS: Here's another one. This time you're Prime Minister, OK? And Amnesty asks you to meet the Dalai Lama to discuss world peace. Or whatever.

RONNIE: The Chinese don't like it.

DARIUS: But if you turn it down, all those
             Guardian readers will write snotty letters. So
             what do you do?

SIMON: I don't know.

RONNIE: You ask the Archbishop of Canterbury
             to sponsor a multi-faith weekend with the Chief
             Rabbi, the Grand Mufti and the Papal Legate
             somewhere in Greater Manchester.

DARIUS: And you go along, and you meet the
             Dalai Lama.

RONNIE: Along with all the rest. And it's a
             spiritual occasion, not a political one.

DARIUS: You sit around talking about the number
             of angels than can dance on the head of a safety
             pin.

RONNIE: The Chinese can live with that.

SIMON: OK, OK. But all these examples…
             (BEAT) you're talking about the *easy* times, the
             long hot summer days of economic boom. But
             when you've actually got a crisis as we have
             now…

DARIUS: Then you've got to talk it up, show
             people you care. But really that's all you can do.

RONNIE: After all, what can you do about the
             credit crunch?

DARIUS: Will it turn out to be a short-lived
             problem, a cold sore maybe, like when the dot-
             com bubble burst?

RONNIE: Or a re-run of the 1929 crash? Long-term leprosy.

SIMON: I don't know.

DARIUS: And neither does anybody else. So what do you do?

RONNIE: Do you start throwing money at the problem? Bailing out the banks? Propping up the pensions? Cutting the interest rates? (BEAT) God, this alliteration thing must be some sort of disease. I think I've caught it off you.

SIMON: Well, yes. (BEAT) I suppose that's what you do. That'll help the companies, safeguard jobs, boost investment.

DARIUS: But then you get inflation, more bad debt, savers start stashing their cash under the bed because they're not getting a decent rate of interest.

RONNIE: Suppose you get a run on the pound? Suppose it falls against the evil Euro?

SIMON: Is that really bad?

DARIUS: Yes it is. But not as bad as a strong pound.

RONNIE: Because that damages exports. (BEAT) Do you offer cheaper mortgages? Help the homeless?

SIMON: I don't know. I think so.

DARIUS: But that keeps house prices unfeasibly high so people can't afford to buy.

RONNIE: And you're just asking for a bigger
            crisis later on.

SIMON: (VERY TROUBLED NOW) Oh God,
            what do we do?

DARIUS: What do we do? *You* tell *us*, Simon.
            You're the man with the words.

RONNIE: In the beginning was the word. And it
            will probably be so at the ending too. The very
            same word, I shouldn't wonder.

DARIUS: Just don't make it sound like an
            unhappy ending, that's all. Keep it happy. For
            us.

RONNIE: Happy for Marcus.

SIMON: I'll do my best.

DARIUS: Of course you will. (BEAT) Look,
            Simon, don't fret. We think you're great. We've
            got no worries about you. None at all.

SIMON: (MORE ENTHUSED NOW) Ok, Ok.

RONNIE: I think we've got him excited again.

DARIUS: As you of course are in the best position
            to verify.

RONNIE: Of course.

LIGHTS DIM STAGE RIGHT THEN COME UP
AGAIN. A SOFA HAS NOW BEEN ADDED TO
TURN DARIUS'S HOTEL ROOM INTO RONNIE'S
HOTEL ROOM. RONNIE AND MARCUS SIT ON

THE SOFA, DARIUS IS SITTING IN A CHAIR TO
THEIR LEFT.

RONNIE: (LEANING FORWARD, PUTTING A
HAND ON MARCUS'S ARM) Don't be
nervous, Marcus.

MARCUS: I'm *not* nervous.

DARIUS: He's got nerves of steel, your husband.

RONNIE: And he's got support.

MARCUS: I hope so.

RONNIE: Everybody in the party with the smallest
smidgin of common sense knows you're the next
leader.

DARIUS: Especially after Plodding Pete's latest
performance.

RONNIE: We believe in you.

MARCUS: (PATS HER HAND) I'm sure you do.
I'm sure what you say is true. And I'm ready to
take my shot, as the Americans say. But I'm
bothered…

DARIUS: (INTERRUPTING) No worries about
Simon, I hope.

MARCUS: No, no. He's a bright young man. Very
bright. Balliol, you know.

DARIUS: Yes, I do.

MARCUS: He's very intelligent. He seems to have an uncanny ability to express all my ideas. As if…

DARIUS: As if they were his own.

MARCUS: Yes. Almost. He's got a great future, that young man.

RONNIE: So what exactly is the problem?

MARCUS: God knows, we're facing a huge crisis. Lots of people didn't like Jack or his policies. But they knew he could win elections. As for me…

DARIUS: You're being too modest. You're the logical successor. There isn't anybody else with the experience…

RONNIE: The track record.

DARIUS: Pete is deputy leader for one reason only. He can talk to the unions in the language they understand: Ancient Moron. There's no way Pete can win a general election. There's no way he could win a lower sixth form debate on whether it sometimes snows at Christmas. A vote for Pete is a vote for defeat.

MARCUS: That's rather good. It rhymes.

RONNIE: But it's not alliterative.

THE BUZZER AT THE DOOR SOUNDS. RONNIE PICKS UP THE REMOTE AND SPEAKS INTO IT

RONNIE: Hello. Who's there?

SIMON: (DISTORTED BY ELECTRONICS)
Simon. And Lorna.

RONNIE: Come and join the party.

SHE PRESSES THE REMOTE AGAIN.
MECHANICAL SOUND OF DOOR OPENING.
MARCUS, DARIUS AND RONNIE TURN THEIR
HEADS TO THE NEWCOMERS WHO ENTER
STAGE RIGHT. RONNIE GETS UP AND WALKS
ACROSS TO THEM

RONNIE: Hello, Lorna. I've heard a lot about you.
In fact, I feel I know you. (LOOKING AT
LORNA'S BELLY) How's the little intruder?

LORNA: As quiet as a burglar.

RONNIE: Be grateful for that. It won't last.

LORNA: You're not the first to tell me that.

DARIUS IS NOW ON HIS FEET. LORNA DARTS A
LOOK AT HIM AS RONNIE MOVES CLOSE TO
SIMON

RONNIE: Hello there, best-selling writer.

SIMON: What have I sold?

RONNIE: I'm sure you're about to do an excellent
job selling Marcus to the assembled hordes.

SIMON: Let's hope so.

RONNIE: Time will tell. (TO GROUP AS A
WHOLE) I'll get some more drinks for people.

DARIUS: *I'll* do it. I know what everybody drinks.

LORNA: (QUICKLY TO DARIUS) I'll come with you. (TO RONNIE) I'll get myself a drink of water out of the tap. Carrying ballast makes you thirsty.

THEY EXIT FROM THE LIGHTED AREA. LIGHTS DIM STAGE RIGHT. LIGHTS COME UP STAGE LEFT. DARIUS AND LORNA KISS BRIEFLY BUT PASSIONATELY. THEN:

LORNA: If you think that means I'm letting you get away with it, think again.

DARIUS: When I was young, you could get a lot for a kiss.

LORNA: Inflation set in a long time ago. Anyway, it never did buy absolution.

DARIUS: And how do you propose I get that? Assuming I believe in the concept?

AS HE TALKS, HE IS BUSTLING AROUND, RE-ARRANGING BOTTLES AND GLASSES ON THE TROLLEY

LORNA: You're a man who can fix anything. I don't want to talk about it. I don't want to hear about difficulties. You're a man who thrives on difficulties. I just don't want this bloody baby.

DARIUS: Ok. I'll fix it. (BEAT) Honest. You'll get all the facilities money can buy. No superbugs. It'll be OK.

LIGHTS DIM STAGE LEFT. LIGHTS GO UP STAGE RIGHT ON RONNIE'S HOTEL LIVING ROOM

AGAIN. ENTER DARIUS WITH DRINKS TROLLEY
AND LORNA, LOOKING DESPONDENT

RONNIE: How was the water?

LORNA: (TAKEN OFF GUARD) Water?
               (BEAT) Oh, fine. You know. (LAMELY)
               Water.

RONNIE: It's just that I could have found you
               some sparkling mineral. Many of these bottled
               waters have surprising medicinal qualities. Good
               for what ails you. I know these things. (BEAT)
               My grandmother was a witch.

DARIUS: We don't do witchcraft in the People's
               Party. Only sleight of hand. (HE STARTS TO
               HAND OUT DRINKS AS THE OTHERS
               GATHER ROUND)

MARCUS: (STILL SAT ON SOFA) Is that what I
               am, Darius? A white rabbit to be pulled out of
               your hat?

DARIUS: You're the white knight, Marcus. Riding
               up on your charger to rescue the injured party.
               Here. Dry Martini.

RONNIE: Don't get him drunk before his big
               moment.

DARIUS: One hour to go. And a perfect moment
               then for you to officially announce your
               candidacy.

MARCUS: A stroke of luck, I suppose. That they'd
               already put me down to speak last. (BEAT)
               Well, there are still only two of us. (BEAT)

Normally, the press would take the early train or be stinking drunk by Friday afternoon.

DARIUS: As it is, they'll be waiting on your every breath. And the stewards will take care of the odd heckler. The security boys always up their game when it's prime minister material they're having to protect. (BEAT) Don't worry. Nobody's going to step out of line. Nobody important. (TO SIMON) Big moment for you too.

SIMON: Oh yes. Hearing the work read out.

DARIUS: More than that. Hearing an orator. A man of charm. A man who understands the power of the word. The power of personality. The choice couldn't be more dramatic. The difference couldn't be more obvious. (BEAT) Let's drink to Marcus. Let's drink to his success.

RONNIE: Let's drink to the party.

ALL: The party. (CLINKING OF GLASSES)

MARCUS: And the party we'll be holding afterwards.

LIGHTS DIM STAGE RIGHT. SPOTLIGHT COMES UP STAGE LEFT. THERE IS SOUND OF APPLAUSE AND CHEERS. ENTER MARCUS, STAGE RIGHT, CLUTCHING SPEECH IN HAND, PROCEEDS TO THE LECTERN STAGE RIGHT AND WAVES FOR APPLAUSE TO CEASE

MARCUS: (ADDRESSING THE AUDIENCE) Now, some people hark back to the past. They say: *You all know my record*. But today I am here to put myself forward as the next leader of our great party and I say: *we know what is past but we do not know the future.* (HE FIDDLES WITH HIS PAPERS)

SPOT COMES ON STAQGE CENTRE REVEALING DARIUS AND SIMON SEATED

DARIUS: Isn't that statement a trifle obvious, Simon? It's hardly the General Theory of Relativity.

SIMON: And how many elections did Einstein ever win?

DARIUS: Point taken.

MARCUS: (ADDRESSING THE AUDIENCE) What is our party really about? It is the moral party. It is the people's party. And I make no apology for punning on the name of our lost leader. It is our tragedy that we face a future without him. But it is also our challenge, our opportunity. We have built in the past few years an enviable economy, a commonwealth in which all members are equal and able to participate, irrespective of sex, race, religion or class. But forces beyond us, forces that batter and buffet our whole planet, have created a situation in which for the first time since 1860, we have endured a run on a British bank. That was the wake-up call. (SHUFFLES HIS PAPERS AGAIN)

DARIUS: Now this I like. We spend all that time creating a great society, with justice, equality and prosperity for all, and what happens? Johnny Foreigner comes along and ruins it. It's somebody else's fault. The Americans. I hope he mentions the Americans. Because everybody in Britain knows everything is America's fault.

SIMON: I didn't want to mention Americans. I thought I'd keep it general, Darius, keep it planetary. So people can make the connection with things like climate change…

DARIUS: I don't follow.

MARCUS: (ADDRESSING AUDIENCE) We need to inject huge sums of money into our economy, we need to kick-start the system that has already made it possible for millions of our people to thrive in unprecedented affluence. We need to create a new opportunity for our voters to continue to buy the luxury goods they have come to regard as their birthright. (BEAT) Some have said this will cost us trillions. Others have said only billions. But today I'm not going to put a figure on the sums involved because I believe passionately that what we need to do, whatever the immediate situation, is react swiftly, and confidently. We need to act *now*! (SHUFFLES HIS PAPERS)

DARIUS: And count the cost after the election. But what about..?

SIMON: Just wait and see.

Marcus: (ADDRESSING AUDIENCE) There are some critics, of course, who say we can't just spend our way out of the credit crisis. That there will come a day of reckoning. But these people are the short-termists who have no vision of the future…

DARIUS: (EXCITED) *Vision*, yes, yes!

Marcus: (ADDRESSING AUDIENCE) I tell those critics that this new policy is not a rejection of that prudence for which this government has become a byword. No. I say this is not a rejection, merely an *in*jection. A temporary means to an end. When the crisis is over, when confidence has returned and we have all begun to enjoy once again that prosperity which is the necessary hallmark of good government, then we can afford to pay back the money we have used to refloat our economy.

HE POSES, SMILING, AS THOUGH ACKNOWLEDGING A PHOTO OPPORTUNITY

DARIUS: Not *re*jection, but *in*jection. Oh, that's good, very good.

SIMON: It's not alliterative, of course, but at least it rhymes.

DARIUS: So debt isn't debt after all, it's just a kind of investment. And spending money is just the same as earning it. But I still don't get the climate change thing.

SIMON: If we're going to be protecting jobs, we can't very well be worrying about cutting our carbon emissions, can we?

DARIUS: No. OK. I see that.

SIMON: So. In the same way that spending and earning are basically the same thing, all part of the same cycle, increasing and decreasing our carbon emissions are also part of a cycle. You can't have one without the other.

DARIUS: Brilliant. I'm astounded. Simon. I think you've finally come of age.

MARCUS: (ADDRESSING THE AUDIENCE)
And it only leaves me to say to the floor, to the party, and ultimately to the electorate, that Marcus Bridgewater is the man to handle the crisis. Thankyou.

MARCUS WAVES, SPOT GOES OFF, FULL LIGHTS COME ON. HE WALKS ACROSS IN FRONT OF DARIUS AND SIMON. THERE IS THUNDEROUS APPLAUSE, LED BY DARIUS AND SIMON SHOUTING AND CLAPPING. MARCUS EXITS STAGE LEFT

DARIUS: Yes, yes, yes! Marcus, you've won them over! Wonderful! You too, Simon!

SIMON: They're only words, Darius.

LIGHTS GO DOWN. AS THE CHEERS FADE, WE HEAR THE THEME MUSIC FOR NEWS AT TEN AND THE VOICE OF A BBC NEWS READER

NEWSREADER: (DISEMBODIED VOICE) And now we go over to 10 Downing Street to hear our new prime minister respond to his election, following his landslide victory among the party membership.

PETE ENTERS INTO SPOT STAGE RIGHT. THIS TIME HE CARRIES A SPIRAL-BOUND SET OF PRINTED PAPERS AND APPEARS MORE CONFIDENT

PETE :   (ADDRESSING AUDIENCE)
Leadership. We must have leadership. We must have decisiveness in the taking of decisions and

the expounding of policy and progression. For
the tasks our leader left us. For that is what the
people expect of the party of the people. That is
why I thank my party for their vote of
confidence. I stood on my record and I stand
here today at the very door of the Prime
Minister's residence, shortly to sit down in the
seat of government. Jack Peeple trusted me to be
his deputy. And that must count for something
of value as we value his opinion. His trust was
not given lightly. Nor should we make light of it
in retrospect. As Jack himself often said: *Trust is
one thing that we can all believe in.* And I trust
that the trust you have now entrusted me with, as
you have bestowed on me the olive branch of
leader, will help me add to the role of leader and
add my name to the roll of honour that is the list
of leaders of our great party. My thanks to all of
you. All of you who voted for me. I can leave
you with no better thought than that. (BEAT)
Thank you.

PETE EXITS STAGE RIGHT FOLLOWED BY SPOT.
MUFFLED APPLAUSE WHICH QUICKLY FADES.
SPOT OFF. LIGHTS GO UP STAGE CENTRE ON
SIMON AND RONNIE IN BED, COVERED BY A
SHEET, THEIR BARE SHOULDERS PROTRUDING

RONNIE: Mmmmm (SNUGGLES UP) And
            mmmmmmmm again. And – why not? –
            mmmmm a third time. I could do with more of
            this sort of thing.

SIMON: (STARING INTO MIDDLE
            DISTANCE) I can't get over it.

RONNIE: I often *do* have that effect on young
            men.

SIMON: (UNRESPONSIVE) No. I mean – poor
             Marcus! How could they do it? How could the
             party end up voting for Pete?

RONNIE: That's politics. Sometimes you lose.
             You have to be relaxed about it.

SIMON: What about Marcus? Is he relaxed?

RONNIE: Marcus has found a new friend.
             Malcolm. A bodybuilder. Tall young man with
             rather lank hair and a bigger chest size than
             mine. (BEAT) And he'll be OK. Marcus, I
             mean. He'll get a peerage in the New Year's. No
             more worrying about votes. (BEAT) Look, the
             party voted for a leader they could throw away.
             We know the party can't win. Not this time
             round. Election in 12 months. Polls plummeting.
             This way the party can blame it on Pete.
             Everybody knows he's a loser. And who wants
             to take over in the middle of a slump anyway?
             You'd have to be mad. (BEAT) On the other
             hand, it gives the real contenders a chance.

SIMON: The *real* contenders?

RONNIE: The ones who need a bit more time to
             make their mark. (BEAT) Your friend Darius,
             for instance. (BEAT) He's made a good start as
             environment minister. He was on News at Ten
             going on about how increasing our carbon
             emissions and decreasing them was all part of
             the same cycle so you couldn't have one without
             the other. It gave me a whole new perspective.
             (BEAT) I'm glad he's got away from all the
             chalk dust and the ASBO generation.

SIMON: (STUNNED) Darius set me up. He set
             Marcus up. And you were part of it. You set me

up to write a speech that would finish Marcus, make him unelectable.

RONNIE: No. Darius thinks a lot of you. (BEAT) And so do I. (SNUGGLES UP TO HIM AGAIN) You wrote a good speech. Full of good ideas. Well, good *words* anyway. (BEAT) If the party's going to lose the next election whatever, it might as well be a Pete sort of loss. So we can clear out the dead wood and start again. So enough people decided to go for the disposable leader. (BEAT) But you, my bold Methodist, are a rising star. You could even be a candidate yourself one of these days. (BEAT) And when I say one of these days, I do mean in the very much long-term. But we *will* be back. We always get back. If there's a world war, we'll still crawl out of the nuclear bunker to get back.

SIMON: No, it's not the waiting that I meant. Look, I'll always be a hack. It's what I'm good at. Lorna's the political one.

RONNIE: (EMBARRASSED) Oh, and I'm sorry. About the other thing. I didn't like to mention it, considering we were… you know…

SIMON: (SIGHS) It's just one of those things that happen in life. But it was all so sudden. Lorna's always prided herself on being careful. Now this! (BEAT) Well, at least it puts politics into perspective. People *do* lose babies. Even today. Even with all the…

RONNIE: …technology.

SIMON: Technology. (BEAT) That's the word.

RONNIE: And you're good with words.

SIMON: Not as good as I thought I was. (BEAT)
            You know, I still rather admire Darius, how his
            mind works.

RONNIE: That's the thing about being a writer.
            You can always afford to be detached. (BEAT)
            But not with me. Not now. I'm suddenly feeling
            a strong urge (SHE KISSES HIM) to be (SHE
            KISSES HIM AGAIN) *attached* once more. I
            hope you do too.

SIMON: Which you, of course, are in the best
            position to verify.

RONNIE: Of course.

THEY BURROW HAPPILY BENEATH THE
BEDCLOTHES. MUSIC: ELGAR'S POMP AND
CIRCUMSTANCE

LIGHTS DIM

END

Luvvies

...began as a 30-minute two-hander in a double bill upstairs in a Wakefield pub. But it didn't work. Then I realised that it wasn't enough to have the "nasty" couple harangue the audience – I had to bring in a second couple to be shouted at. This version was finally produced by the **ActONE** company in Leeds. Cast and crew:

Steve...Paul Newell
Caroline...Linda Edwards
Andy...Warwick St John
Sofi...Emma Hewitt

Directed by Marian Mantovani
Stage Manager: Christi Hetzler
Technician: Peter Meese
Running time: 60 minutes

Characters:

Steve, a middle-aged over-the-top ad man and failed playwright
Caroline, a middle-aged actress, married to Steve
Andy, a young, award-winning TV writer
Sofi, an even younger, naïve drama student, living with Andy

Time: The present
Scene: The living room of the house belonging to Steve and Caroline somewhere in the south of England

Props and furniture: Sofa, two chairs, small table, telephone, telephone book, bottle of whisky, four whisky glasses, a tray, a Samuel French copy of Joe Orton's *Funeral Games*, a glossy colour A4 photograph of Caroline.

Costume: The men appear in smart suits or dinner jackets, the women in evening gowns.

STAGE IN DARKNESS. SOUND EFFECTS OF A
PARTY – BABBLE OF VOICES, CLINKING OF
GLASSES, LAUGHTER

CAROLINE: (DISEMBODIED VOICE, ANGRY
                AND SCARED): I don't care what you think,
                Steve! I don't care any more!

STEVE: (DISEMBODIED VOICE, ANGRY)
                Caroline! You bitch! You lying, cheating bitch!

SOUND OF LOUD SLAP FOLLOWED BY
WOMAN'S HIGH-PITCHED SQUEAL

STEVE: (DISEMBODIED VOICE, NOW A
                STAGE WHISPER) Oh God, I'm sorry. (BEAT)
                Look. Those friends of yours are coming over
                here.

CAROLINE: (DISEMBODIED VOICE, ALSO A
                WHISPER, SOBBING) *What* friends?

STEVE: (DISEMBODIED VOICE) They're
                coming over, whoever they are! (BEAT) Stop
                your bloody waterworks. (BEAT) Come on,
                Caroline. You're supposed to be an actress.

CAROLINE: (DISEMBODIED VOICE) They're no
                friends of mine.

STEVE: (DISEMBODIED VOICE) They're
                coming over anyway! *Act* as if they're your
                friends!

ANDY: (DISEMBODIED VOICE) Hi. Hello. Hi
                there.

STEVE :   (DISEMBODIED VOICE) Hello.

CAROLINE: (DISEMBODIED VOICE, HOLDING BACK THE SOBS NOW) Hello. Hi.

SOFI: (DISEMBODIED VOICE) I'm Sofi. This is Andy, my guy. (LAUGHS) We just thought we'd…

ANDY: (DISEMBODIED VOICE) …come over, say hello. (BEAT) Are you OK?

SOFI: (DISEMBODIED VOICE) Is there something in your eye?

CAROLINE: (DISEMBODIED VOICE) No, no. it's just that…

STEVE: (DISEMBODIED VOICE) She always blubs on these occasions. Loves award ceremonies. (BEAT) Don't you, dear? Caroline loves to hear gratitude publicly expressed. It's an emotional high for her.

ANDY: (DISEMBODIED VOICE) It *can* be very emotional.

STEVE: (DISEMBODIED VOICE) Especially for *you*, Michael. (BEAT) You think I didn't recognise you.

ANDY: (DISEMBODIED VOICE) No. It's Andy. My name is Andy.

STEVE: (DISEMBODIED VOICE) Yes. But tonight you're Mr Winner.

ANDY: (DISEMBODIED VOICE) Sorry?

STEVE: (DISEMBODIED VOICE) TV writer of the year. Best drama series.

SOFI: (DISEMBODIED VOICE) He's making a joke, my love. Michael *Winner*. (LAUGHS)

STEVE: (DISEMBODIED VOICE, SCATHING) Get it?

ANDY :   (DISEMBODIED VOICE) Oh. Yes. (LAUGHS) Michael Winner. Yes, that's very good. Very good.

THEY ALL LAUGH. THEN A BRIEF SILENCE AFTER WHICH THE LIGHTS GO UP ON THE LIVING ROOM WITH A SOFA STAGE RIGHT; A TABLE WITH A PHONE BOOK, A BOTTLE OF WHISKY, AN A4 SIZE PHOTO AND A PLAY BOOK ON IT, CENTRE; TWO CHAIRS STAGE LEFT. STEVE, CAROLINE, ANDY AND SOFI ENTER STAGE LEFT. THE MEN ARE OBVIOUSLY DRUNK AND FULL OF CAMARADERIE, THE WOMEN STILL SOBER AND UNEASY, CARRYING HANDBAGS.

SOFI: (LOOKING ROUND WITH EXAGGERATED POLITENESS) Gosh, this is nice.

SHE PLACES HER HANDBAG ON THE TABLE. CAROLINE DROPS HERS ON THE SOFA

STEVE: (SARCASTICALLY) Nice. Yes. *We* like to think it is. Well, it's our home. Our little love nest, Caroline and me. (BEAT) Nice. That's a good word. A *nice* word. Don't you think so, Andy?

ANDY: (MORE OBVIOUSLY DRUNK THAN STEVE) What?

STEVE: You're the man of words. The wordsmith. What's going on in your smithy at the moment?

ANDY: Well, I…

STEVE: No, *don't* tell us. Keep some trade secrets. *I* do. I don't go around telling people the tricks of *my* trade. Why should I? Let them find their own trade.

ANDY: I know what you mean. (BEAT) You're in *advertising*, aren't you?

STEVE: Yes. (BEAT) But I used to be a writer. I used to write plays. Only amateur stuff. The Pricklington Players present a one-act festival of new local writing. That sort of thing.

CAROLINE: (NODDING) That's how he met me. I was his first leading lady.

STEVE: She was an amateur then like the rest of us. But she got herself an agent. And now she's everybody's leading lady… *Everybody's*! I don't exaggerate!

CAROLINE: (GIVES HIM A HARD LOOK THEN LAUGHS) Today Pricklington, tomorrow the world.

ANDY: My girlfriend's an actress too.

SOFI: (EMBARRASSED) Well… I'm still at drama school. College. I started late. But I *want* to be an actress.

STEVE: (TO ANDY AND SOFI) Why don't I tell you about some of my plays? You're obviously lovers of drama, so I'm sure you'll enjoy the experience.

CAROLINE: (QUICKLY TO SOFI AND ANDY) No, you won't! But that won't stop him. (BEAT) They were always about *lurve*. L-U-R-V-E! There was always this young man. He was very idealistic. Deeply sensitive. He hated social injustice. He used to march a lot.

STEVE: (STARTS MARCHING ON THE SPOT) March, march, march! Ban *this*! Stop *that*! Feed *them*! (BEAT) This young man, he used to meet a lot of girls on these marches. And he would always end up meeting this very special girl. And she was just as soft and sensitive as he was.

CAROLINE: And Bingo! They went to bed. (BEAT) Would you believe it!

STEVE: And they enjoyed it. I mean, they *both* enjoyed it.

CAROLINE: Which, to my way of thinking, is a very rare occurrence. In *real* life, anyway.

SOFI: So what happened to them in the end?

STEVE: Nothing much. (BEAT) Actually, if I'm honest, all the marches and the demos and the hatred of social injustice, all this turned out to be the scenery. And that's the difference between theatre and life. In a play, they change the scenery, but the characters remain.

CAROLINE: In real life, only the scenery stays the same.

STEVE: In real life the deeply sensitive young man goes into advertising.

CAROLINE: He becomes a copywriter.

SOFI: (TRYING TO SHOW POLITE INTEREST) What were you saying about tricks of the trade?

STEVE: (THINKS) Oh yes. (BEAT) When you're a writer, any kind of writer, you've only got to meet some chap in a bar. Or he might be standing next to you at the urinals...

CAROLINE: I'm very suspicious about men and urinals.

STEVE: And as soon as you tell him what you do, as soon as you admit to being a writer...

ANDY: Right...

STEVE: ...you can bet he'll always say: *Oh, I do a bit of writing myself.*

ANDY: (LAUGHS) A bit of writing! (BEAT) Hell!

STEVE: That's what they say. And then they say: *I actually thought of taking it up at one time. Professionally.*

ANDY: (LAUGHS) Professionally!

STEVE: And then they say: All that stuff on TV. It's all rubbish. Anybody could write that.

ANDY: (LAUGHS) Rubbish! (THEN RECONSIDERS) Oh no, some of it's actually pretty good.

SOFI: Don't get upset, Andy. Steve's only quoting some... *gent*!

STEVE: Some gent. In a gents. Unless it's a woman. (BEAT) Then they say...

CAROLINE: (INTERRUPTING) I don't think you're going to meet many women in the gents.

SHE GLANCES AT SOFI AND THEY BOTH LAUGH. CAROLINE TURNS AGAIN TO STEVE

CAROLINE: Oh, I know you think you're still a writer. Even if you've never won anything. (BEAT) Unlike Andy, who did *very* well tonight. (BEAT) And I know you probably have a smart answer, a dramatic device, a back-story, a plot development, that would make it somehow plausible that you are standing next to a woman in the gents. (TURNS TO SOFI) Funny word *urinals*. For many years I thought it was a mountain range in Russia.

SOFI LAUGHS AGAIN. CAROLINE TURNS AGAIN TO STEVE

CAROLINE: But I have to say I find it implausible that you would ever be in such an intimate situation with any person of the female persuasion...

ANDY: (DEFENDING STEVE) Now, now, I think we've shifted scene here, that's what I think we've done. I don't think Steve is really suggesting...

STEVE: (QUICKLY) That's Ok, Andy. I can defend myself, thank you very much. (BEAT) So, yes, he's right. The award-winning young writer is right. We shift our scene to the kitchen or the jacuzzi or the boudoir or wherever you want to situate this comedy of manners…

ANDY: You have a jacuzzi?

CAROLINE: Don't be stupid. We don't even have a flush that works properly.

STEVE: (TO CAROLINE) I plan to continue regardless with this evening's performance, Caroline, love of my life, because, it seems to me, we *do* have a friendly audience. (INDICATES ANDY AND SOFI) Even if there's only *two* of them.

CAROLINE: A *select* audience. That's what we used to say when the actors outnumbered the audience. (BEAT) The show must go on.

STEVE: The show must go on. (TO ANDY AND SOFI) And if it's a woman, wherever she happens to be standing, moved by whatever plot device, she will probably say: (PUTS ON GIRLY VOICE) *Oh, the things I write are so personal, you know. I couldn't possibly let anyone else read them. I'm too sensitive.* (BEAT) There. That's women for you. Sensitive. (BEAT) As sensitive as a condom stuffed with broken glass.

ANDY: That's good.

STEVE: What is?

95

ANDY: (SUDDENLY EMBARRASSED) What you said. A condom… you know…

SOFI: (ANNOYED) Andy, you've had a lot to drink tonight.

STEVE: But still not enough. There are times in life when you just have to celebrate and this is one of them. (TO CAROLINE) Did we put the champagne on ice, my love? (BEAT) No? Oh dear, then we'll just have to do with the usual rotgut. (TURNS TOWARDS THE BOTTLE ON THE TABLE) And here it is! At our disposal! Fate smiles down on us! The booze *ex machina*! (TO CAROLINE) Would you care to bring in the glasses, my angel? It will give you a chance to show Sindy..

SOFI: (INTERRUPTING) Sofi.

STEVE: Sofi. (BEAT) It will give you a chance to show *Sofi* the *salle de cuisine*.

ANDY: Kitchen!

STEVE: That *is* the translation.

SOFI: *We've* just had a new kitchen.

ANDY: Stainless steel sink. (BEAT) And you know what?

STEVE: What?

ANDY: It came with two leaflets. The stainless steel sink. One leaflet was about how to prevent stains. And the other one told you how to remove the stains when they happened anyway.

HE LOOKS ROUND GRINNING. NOBODY
REACTS.

ANDY: (FORCED TO EXPLAIN) It's a
     stainless steel sink, right? And there are two
     leaflets...

SOFI: We get it.

ANDY: I mean, what is the English language
     coming to when you can have a stainless steel
     sink...

STEVE: So-called.

ANDY: So called. And you get two leaflets...

SOFI: (QUICKLY TO CAROLINE) Gosh. I
     think I would like to see your kitchen *now*.

ANDY :   Hell. I blame the advertising industry.
     They've permanently damaged the language of
     Shakespeare.

SOFI: (TO ANDY) Steve's in advertising.
     Remember?

ANDY: (EMBARRASSED) Ah, yes.

CAROLINE: The only reason he was at the ceremony
     tonight was that his agency wanted him to talk to
     everyone, make contacts with successful people.
     Even if it's only for a single night. (TO SOFI)
     Yes, let's get some glasses. I can see we're in for
     a *brilliant* evening.

SHE SHEPHERDS SOFI OFF STAGE LEFT

ANDY: (TO STEVE) I didn't mean...

STEVE: What?

ANDY: About advertising. I didn't mean to slag
off the advertising industry.

STEVE: Don't let it worry you. Everybody
makes cracks about the advertising game.

ANDY: No, no. You ads people pay the bills for
us *creative* people. Anyway, lots of talented
people come up through advertising. (BEAT)
Salman Rushdie…

STEVE: But *I* haven't…

ANDY: What?`

STEVE: …come up through. Not yet. (BEAT)
But that's enough about *me*. Tell me about *you*.

ANDY: There's not much…

STEVE: … to tell? Try. Try *hard*. Words are
your business.

ANDY: I graduated from drama school eight
years ago. And I thought: *God, there's so many
of us. Actors, writers…*

STEVE: Writers, actors…

STEVE GOES OVER TO TABLE, PICKS UP PHOTO,
STUDIES IT, THROWS IT ON THE FLOOR

ANDY: But I had this friend. Jocelyn
Burberry…

STEVE: *School*friend?

ANDY: Yes.

STEVE: *Public* school?

ANDY: Yes.

STEVE: Harrow or Eton?

ANDY: Winchester. I'm an old Wykehamist

STEVE: *School*friends. They're the best kind. Last a lifetime, guaranteed. And Jocelyn is a good name. It has the ring of sincerity.

ANDY: ...who worked for the BBC. I sent him an e-mail. Thought it was worth a try. You know, to tell him I was available. And he e-mailed me back and then...

STEVE: You met for a pint of real ale. And reminisced about simple pleasures on the playing fields...

ANDY: Well...

STEVE: Everyone has a favourite story about scrumming down.

ANDY: And he told me about his new series. Sort of like *Day of the Triffids*, but updated to give it a modern resonance. *Eco-crash*.

STEVE: *Eco-crash*. Yes, I remember Jonathan Ross mentioning the title before they opened the envelope and your name came tumbling out.

ANDY: Same idea as the *Triffids*. But none of this *extraterrestrial* stuff.

STEVE: ET just isn't PC, is he? And you wouldn't want to cast any fruit or vegetables in an unsympathetic role. It might damage the five-portions-a-day campaign.

ANDY: This time it's the human race that causes the catastrophe. Capitalism. Globalisation. America.

STEVE: The usual suspects. I see the drift.

ANDY: So the holocaust happens. Only this time it's *mega*holocaust.

STEVE: The new improved version. (BEAT) That's the advertising talking.

ANDY: And nearly everybody's wiped out. (BEAT) Am I boring you with this?

STEVE: Such is my enthusiasm for life and literature that I do not know the meaning of the word *boredom*. Though I'm always willing to learn.

ANDY: (AMAZED) So all this really is new to you? You've never actually seen the show?

STEVE: Something happened to our TV a little while ago. I think the digital recorder and the wrap-around sound stopped talking to each other. Just a small family squabble in the great world of electronics. But we've been cut off from traditional conduits of culture for several months.

ANDY: Well, OK. So we've got modern multicultural Britain in the grip of ecological disaster. Imagine it. Breakdown of services.

Collapse of law and order. But a few survive.
Strangers thrown together by catastrophe.
Different races, different creeds…

STEVE: Both *sexes*, I hope. Otherwise there
might not be a second series.

ANDY: Oh yes. Both *sexes*. You see, Jocelyn
said to me very early on that it had to be up-to-
the-minute and reflect contemporary reality…

STEVE: In a futuristic way.

ANDY: Yes. And Jocelyn said to me: *did I know
how we should handle it?*

STEVE: And I bet you did.

ANDY: Well, I thought: *let's get away from
ethnic stereotypes for a start.*

STEVE: Bravo.

ANDY: And let's have more women taking on
stronger roles.

STEVE: Feisty females. The mind fairly boggles.
(BEAT) Which reminds me. Aren't girls funny?
And I *do* mean girls, I don't mean women. I *do*
know the difference. Women aren't funny. Not
to me. But girls are so *soft*. They make out they
want a man who's as soft as *they* are. But they
don't. It's just a phase they go through. What
they actually want is to be actresses. Actresses!
You can have 'em as far as *I'm* concerned!

ANDY: (PUT OUT) My girlfriend's an actress.
Well, she's *trying* to be. Remember?

STEVE: Sorry. (BEAT) Of course, my wife is as well. (BEAT) Tell me more about *Echo Beach*.

ANDY: *Eco-crash*.

STEVE: Of course. It's just that they sound a bit similar.

ANDY: Well, another idea I had was that maybe it could reflect the credit crunch and the war in Iraq in an allegorical way.

STEVE: Putting the gore into alle*gory*. Which I'm sure it does. And here you are – a winner!

ANDY: (GRINS) It feels good. (BEAT) But the thing is…

ANDY STEPS BACK AND SUDDENLY LOOKS DOWN

ANDY: What's this?

HE PEELS THE PHOTO OF CAROLINE OFF THE SOLE OF HIS SHOE

STEVE: (TAKING THE PHOTO FROM HIM) It's Caroline. It's one of her publicity shots. Don't you recognise her?

ANDY: (GUILTY) I didn't mean to…

STEVE: Disrespect her? Of course not. (BEAT) Don't worry about stepping on her face. Men have done far worse things than that to Caroline. *And* in her face. *And* she's enjoyed it. (HE HANDS BACK THE PICTURE) There. Have a good look. I bet you could tell she was an actress the moment you met her.

ANDY: Well…

STEVE: Of course you could. I bet the moment
           you set eyes on her you said: *This is an actress.
           This is her in the flesh.* (BEAT) Sorry. *She* in the
           flesh. Since I know you care about the English
           language.

ANDY: Did I actually say that?

STEVE: You only need to meet her the once and
           you can see what she is. It's the soft focus that
           gives it away. She's one of those people who
           carry soft focus around with them. (BEAT) And
           she rehearses a lot. At home. I often say to her:
           *Go on, my love, do your poses. Do demure. Do
           heartbreak. Oh, look at that! Now do angry.*

ANDY: Is she good at angry?

STEVE: Not as good as *I* am. *I'm* the one who
           usually does angry. I'm very natural. (BEAT) I
           used to be an actor before I became a writer.
           Amateur, again.

ANDY: Before you went into advertising.

STEVE: So you can say I know a bit about
           acting. That's what gives me the expertise to be
           angry. (BEAT) And I'll tell you one thing that
           makes me *really* angry. It's when the actors talk
           to the audience. The actors aren't *there* to talk to
           the audience. They're there to talk to each other.
           And the audience, well, they're supposed to
           listen…

ANDY: (NODS) Eavesdrop!

STEVE: ...pick up what it's all about from what's going on. That's the *job* of the audience. If I had an audience here right now – I mean a *proper* audience – you know what I'd say to them?

ANDY: No.

STEVE: If *you* were my audience, I'd say to you (RAISES VOICE) *That's what you're doing now. Listening. Doing your job! I hope you feel satisfied with your employment.* (BACK TO NORMAL VOICE) It just makes me mad when the actors talk to the audience. That John Godber, he's the worst. And William Shakespeare. *Hamlet*, for God's sake! Soliloquies. Talking to the audience all the bloody time. Jabber, jabber, jabber. *What a piece of work is this*! No bloody piece at all, I'd say! I wouldn't give that William Shakespeare a pot to piss in. No. Really. I wouldn't.

STEVE GOES ACROSS TO ANDY, TAKES THE PHOTO AWAY FROM HIM, LOOKS AT IT, HOLDS IT HIGH SO THE REAL AUDIENCE CAN SEE IT

STEVE: Publicity shots. It's just a form of advertising. It's what actresses need. Glossy, smart, seductive. Nice word *seductive.* If you like words of three syllables. It's like calling knickers *lingerie.*

ANDY: (SIGHS DRUNKENLY) Ah. Lingerie. Models...

STEVE: You know what? Models who advertise knickers are more honest than actresses. What's a model got, eh? Just the body she stands up in and the face that she smiles at you with. She puts on the knickers. She says..

ANDY: (PUTS ON A GIRLY VOICE) *Buy my knickers.*

STEVE: And some bloke sees the picture in a magazine. Or at a bus stop. And it makes him feel good. Just for a second. And he smiles. And he says: *I'll buy my wife a pair like that.*

ANDY: If he's *married.*

STEVE: (LAUGHS SARCASTICALLY) *If he's married*! Nice one. Just the sort of point that might come up at the script conference. (BEAT) So that's what a model does. Makes a bloke feel good. Sells knickers. Keeps the economy moving along very nicely. Models are fine by me. (BEAT) But actresses! God! What do actresses advertise? Themselves! That's the difference between acting and advertising

ANDY: Salman Rushdie...

STEVE: ...came up through it. I know! But *I* didn't. (BEAT) If I had that audience here now, you know what I'd say to them? I'd say (ADDRESSES REAL AUDIENCE AGAIN) If there's anybody wants to make something out of that, any left-wing loonie out there in the audience who doesn't like advertising, if there's anybody like that in this theatre tonight... well, I've got news for him. Advertising is *honest.*

ANDY: (SEEING HIS CHANCE) Look, hold on a bit. We may have got off on the wrong foot here. I don't want you to think that I'm unappreciative of what advertising can do. (BEAT) Take Sofi for instance.

STEVE: I thought you already had.

ANDY: She's a bit younger than me. And very idealistic. Loves theatre. Smell of the greasepaint, that sort of thing. But it's hard out there, God knows.

STEVE: A jungle.

ANDY: And I think she's got a brilliant face for TV. For commercials. I'm sure she could do all that lingerie stuff you were talking about. And not just that, but anything that's female with a capital F. Tampons, health foods, slimmers' meals, those bacteria drinks that keep their vaginas clean…

STEVE: And washing powders, fast food, lavatory cleaners. Yes, I'm sure she could.

ANDY: Could you fix that? They pointed you out to me tonight as somebody who might be very useful.

STEVE: Did they? Well, I might *try*. We don't want poor Sofi dying on stage, do we? Just for a lie. That's what theatre is, dear boy, just a lie.

HE COLLAPSES ON TO THE SOFA AND THROWS THE PICTURE BACK ON THE FLOOR. SUDDENLY HIS HEAD LOLLS BACK, HE SLUMPS AND BEGINS TO SNORE

ANDY: (REALLY CARRIED AWAY NOW, SO HE DOESN'T NOTICE) Was it Baudelaire who said *Theatre is the expression of truth through the medium of a lie*? (BEAT) Or was it Nietsche?

HE STUMBLES, FALLS OVER AND LIES ON HIS
ELBOW ON THE FLOOR. A MINUTE LATER
CAROLINE AND SOFI RE-ENTER STAGE LEFT.
CAROLINE IS CARRYING A TRAY OF GLASSES

SOFI: *Our* sink is really very good. I wouldn't
want you to think it wasn't. After what Andy
said... (SHE SEES HIM ON THE FLOOR) Oh
God, what's happened?

SOFI RUSHES OVER TO THE FALLEN ANDY,
CAROLINE WALKS AT A MORE MEASURED
PACE, DEPOSITS THE TRAY ON THE TABLE AND
STROLLS ACROSS TO THE SOFA WHERE STEVE
IS NOW SNORING

SOFI: Oh, Andy, you're not usually like this.

ANDY: (GRINNING) Hell. Like what?

CAROLINE: (INSPECTING STEVE) I hope you've
got the idea by now, you two. I hope you can *see*
what it's really like in my marriage.

SHE GOES ACROSS TO ANDY AND SHE AND
SOFI HELP HIM INTO ONE OF THE CHAIRS

ANDY: I'm OK. (BEAT) I'm a winner.

SOFI: Well, you're not having any more to
drink. (TO CAROLINE) I'm so ashamed. We've
only just met you.

CAROLINE: Don't be ashamed. *You're* the one that
got the winner. Let *me* be ashamed. (BEAT)
Look, *we're* not pissed out of our minds, you
and me. I think we deserve a little something.

SHE POURS TWO SHOTS OF WHISKY AND
HANDS ONE TO SOFI, WHO HESITATES, THEN:

SOFI: Ok. Why not? (TO CAROLINE)
          Cheers!

ANDY: Cheers. (HE RAISES AN EMPTY
          FIST)

SOFI: (GLANCING ACROSS AT STEVE)
          Your husband must be really fast asleep.

CAROLINE: Who knows? One thing I've learned
          about Steve is never assume he's ever what he
          seems to be. Sometimes he pretends to switch
          off. So never think for a minute when he's lying
          in that chair, snoring like a pig, which he does a
          lot of the time, that he's really asleep.

SOFI: (SHOCKED) You're joking!

CAROLINE: (LAUGHS) I never joke about Steve.
          (BEAT) Seriously, I've made that sort of
          mistake before. I've paid a lot for thinking that
          when he says: *Let's be honest with each other,*
          that he really wants to be honest.

SOFI: Why does he say it then?

CAROLINE: Why? Because Steve and the truth are
          like chalk and gorgonzola.

CAROLINE SITS NEXT TO STEVE ON THE SOFA,
THEN PICKS UP THE PLAY BOOK FROM THE
TABLE AND GLANCES AT IT. SOFI SITS ON THE
CHAIR NEXT TO ANDY'S CHAIR.

SOFI: (POINTING EXCITEDLY TO THE
          PLAY BOOK) You've got a script! You're

working then? You're not resting or anything? What is it?

CAROLINE: *Funeral Games* by Joe Orton. (BEAT) Sorry. I didn't mean to be rude. (SHE PUTS THE PLAY BOOK BACK ON THE TABLE)

SOFI: No, it's OK. It's exciting. Being an actress. That's what I'm trying to be.

CAROLINE: (ROLLING HER EYES) Yes, I know. Good God, what brought on this madness?

SOFI: I suppose it was my mum. She used to do *am dram*. She was called Miriam Broadbent – she kept her maiden name for stage work. She was with something called Thornley Little Theatre. In Weymouth. And she's still with them, after all these years, even if all she gets to do nowadays is prompt. And she's done all the classic roles, all the great women's parts (LAUGHS) if that's not a vulgar expression. (BEAT) Beatrice, Rosalind, Lady Macbeth, Alison Porter, Blanche DuBois. You know what she told me? She said the one regret of her life was that when she did Juliet, she hadn't acquired the emotional depth – that's how she put it. And now she'd got the experience, she was too old to play it. I ask you! My mum's a filing clerk at the Weymouth Building Society!

CAROLINE: (LAUGHS) Well, all the world's a stage…

SOFI: And if you're an actress, you've got the whole world at your feet. Even Weymouth.

CAROLINE: And what do you think they're doing at your feet? Looking up your skirt.

SOFI: (SHOCKED) Ooh, that's *so* cynical.

CAROLINE: So. You really want to be an actress. But you're not out of college yet?

SOFI: I graduate this year. I've done lots of student things. I was Sally Bowles in *Cabaret*.

CAROLINE: You sing too? I wish *I* could sing.

SOFI: Gosh. I don't really sing. I just sort of talk it in a high-pitched voice. (STARTS TO SING) *Money makes the world go round, the world go round, the world go round...*

CAROLINE: No. That's *singing*. That's *real* singing.

SOFI: (PLEASED) Do you think so?

CAROLINE: As much as Leonard Cohen does singing.

SOFI: (STILL PLEASED) Oh thanks.

CAROLINE: So. What else have you done?

SOFI: I was Hedda Gabler at the end of my third term.

CAROLINE: Oh, that's a brilliant part.

SOFI: I don't know. I found it difficult. All that boy stuff. Guns. I can't connect to guns.

CAROLINE: I bet you're a vegetarian as well.

SOFI: Yes, I am, as a matter of fact. I think it all starts with what you eat. If you reverence life, you don't want to eat anything that's ever been a living creature, do you? So you don't. And then, I believe you *are* what you eat, so…

CAROLINE: If you don't eat animals to begin with, you won't *want* to eat animals because it's eating animals in the first place that gives you the habit.

SOFI: Yes! Absolutely! I think you're the first person I've ever explained it to who actually *understood* it.

SUDDENLY ANDY STARTS IN HIS CHAIR, SITS UP, PUTS A HAND TO HIS MOUTH, STARTS TO BELCH AND SPLUTTER

SOFI: Oh my God! Andy! Andy! (TO CAROLINE) Where's your loo?

CAROLINE: Top of the stairs. You can't miss it. We always leave the door open. (BEAT) I mean when there's nobody in there, of course.

CAROLINE GETS UP, HELPS SOFI SUPPORT A GURGLING ANDY AS HE IS LED OFF STAGE LEFT. SOUNDS OF FEET GOING UPSTAIRS. THEN CAROLINE RE-ENTERS,TURNS BACK TO THE SOFA, WALKS ROUND IT, STUDIES THE SNORING STEVE INTENTLY, SITS DOWN NEXT TO HIM, RUBS HER EYES, KICKS OFF HER SHOES, RUBS HER TOES, PICKS UP HER HANDBAG, TAKES OUT A MIRROR, LOOKS AT HER FACE, STUDIES HER EYES, PUTS MIRROR AWAY. AFTER A MINUTE OR SO, SOFI RE-ENTERS STAGE LEFT

DURING THE NEXT SECTION THERE IS A SENSE OF CAROLINE AND SOFI ESTABLISHING

RAPPORT, EVEN FRIENDSHIP, AS THEY TALK
ABOUT THEIR COMMON EXPERIENCE

SOFI: I left him in there. I think it's better he's
alone right now. God, men are such pigs! I told
him to clean up afterwards. (BEAT) If he
doesn't, I'll go back and…

DISTANT SOUNDS OF VOMITING

CAROLINE: No, you won't. (BEAT) I'm sure he's
house-trained.

SOFI: He's really disgraced himself tonight.

CAROLINE: No, he hasn't. He's just being foolish,
letting it go to his head. (BEAT) You want
disgrace? I'll tell you about disgrace! (SHE
POINTS TO HER EYE) Take a good look.
Steve gave me this. Tonight. Because his name
wasn't in the envelope. Or any other envelope
for that matter.

SOFI: (SHOCKED) He hit you? Oh no!

CAROLINE: It's not the first time either. OK, I know
you can't see it properly now. That's because of
the make-up. Little bit of feminine artifice. And
I'm not going to wash it off just to show you
what he did to me. You know why? I'm
ashamed.

SOFI: You're very brave.

CAROLINE: I'm just a good actress. (BEAT). God
knows, there's not a lot you can say for being an
actress. Most of the time it's: *Do it this way.*
Say it like this. Say it differently, say it better,
smile, don't smile, don't be self-conscious.

SOFI: Don't be self-conscious! (LAUGHS) That's a good one.

CAROLINE: The director who said that to me was trying to get me to take my top off. I did in the end. But it didn't get me the part. Anyway, the girl who got the part... whatever happened to her? Nothing, that's what. She's probably still going to auditions, taking her top off, living in hope.

SOFI: I dread being asked to take my top off.

CAROLINE: At least for me, the work's regular. A bit of touring. Radio commercials. (IN RADIO VOICE) Girls, do you suffer from irregular periods? (BEAT) Ladies, are you getting a quality deal from your current car insurance? (IN NORMAL VOICE) It gets me out of the house. It gets me away from that. (INDICATES STEVE)

SOFI: I like the idea of radio. They'd never ask you to take your top off for radio, would they?

CAROLINE: And I've done TV. *The Bill*. I had to unlock a cell door. *Wire in the Blood*. I was a bloated corpse floating down-river. (LAUGHS) Type-casting. (BEAT) And I was in *Corrie*. Some years ago, mind. In The Rovers Return. I was the one coming out of the toilets when Vera Duckworth had her fainting fit. (BEAT) I was touring once with (BEAT) what's her name? She was in *Eastenders* for years. Then she turned up in *Footballer's Wives*. Or was it *Midsomer Murders*? Oh, it's gone. That's terrible, that is. Forgetting somebody's name is almost as bad as forgetting your lines. Anyway, it was *The Doll's House*. The play that we toured in.

SOFI: Oh, you've done Ibsen too! Like me.

CAROLINE: I was only the maid. She was The Doll. I like to think all those people came for my maid (IN AFFECTED VOICE) *Ooh, you must see The Doll's House when it comes to the Playhouse! Ooh, that maid! She's not got much to say, but she's got such presence.*

CAROLINE SUDDENLY SEES HER PICTURE ON THE FLOOR. SHE WALKS ACROSS, PICKS IT UP, HANDS IT TO SOFI, THEN SITS DOWN AGAIN.

SOFI: (LOOKING AT PHOTO) Oh yes, very nice.

CAROLINE: You know, sometimes I look at my pictures, my publicity shots, and I think *who is it*? Steve says it's not the picture that's the problem.

SOFI: What's the problem then?

CAROLINE: Steve says: *I'm* the problem. He says I'm not really asking *Who is it*? I'm asking: *Who am I*? And he thinks he's got the answer to that one. (BEAT) But I won't tell you what his answer is.

SOFI: (PUTTING PICTURE ON TABLE AND PICKING UP PLAY BOOK) I have to say I don't really like Joe Orton. And it's the one where they tie up this woman, isn't it? Gives me shivers, that does. (PUTS BOOK DOWN AGAIN) *I* don't want to be tied up on stage. I like a part that has *movement*. (SHE WAVES

HER ARMS ABOUT)   But I'm that sort of actress. Expressive.

CAROLINE: Well, I know I should still be going over it. Looking for subtext. But you can only get through so much before your mind goes a blank. And then you can't see the joke. You might be reading a very funny script. And suddenly it's not funny any more. That's when you know you've had enough.

SOFI: I know what you mean. You have to take a rest. (BEAT) Resting. That's not a word I like. It's not a healthy word. Not for actors, it isn't.

SUDDENLY STEVE EMITS A PARTICULARLY LOUD SNORE

CAROLINE: (LOOKS ACROSS AT STEVE) What is it about people when they're asleep? (TO STEVE LOUDLY) Or *pretending* to sleep? Did you hear that, Steve? Did you think you were fooling me? (WAITS FOR REACTION BUT GETS NONE, TURNS AGAIN TO SOFI)

SOFI: You're very suspicious. (BEAT) At least I know Andy's really *sick*. You can't pretend something like vomit.

CAROLINE: Steve's had a lot more than I thought. (BEAT) It's the worst thing for an actor. Not the drink. I mean, drinking is bad enough. But no. What I meant was: playing someone who's asleep. That's the worst thing, the most difficult.

SOFI: No, no! I'll tell you something that's worse and that's playing somebody who's dead! Because you lie there, trying not to move a muscle and you want to blink, and you get cramps and you want to sneeze and you start to itch. (BEAT) I always start to itch in the most embarrassing places. At least when you're asleep, you can breathe. You can even move a bit and it's still ok.

CAROLINE: (INTERESTED NOW) Well, if you're making lists, I'll tell you a *few* other things that are difficult. *Love* scenes for a start. They never look real, do they? *You're* a woman. Let me ask you. Because the men will never give you a straight answer. (BEAT) When I'm watching other people in love scenes I'm always thinking: *she wouldn't do that really*. And I'm thinking: *he's only turned that way because his right profile isn't as good as his left*.

SOFI: And *she's* trying to hide her nipples under the duvet. No, you're right. I can't take it seriously.

CAROLINE: Mind you, these days I can't take it seriously in real life either. Not in *my* marriage. I think: I wouldn't do *that* – not if I was enjoying it. And I'm thinking: *Christ, what's the use? Why don't we just bring down the curtain?* (SHOUTS ACROSS AT STEVE) Did you hear that Steve? (TURNS AGAIN TO SOFI) What else is hard?

SOFI: Laughing. I can never laugh on cue. I always try to memorise a joke before the show. But when it's my turn to laugh, I can never remember the punchline.

CAROLINE: What about crying? Nothing works with crying, does it? Trying to remember something sad never makes you cry, it just makes you trip over the furniture.

SOFI: Sometimes when I'm on stage, I might look very relaxed, but I'm listening to the audience. The little cough, the whisper...

CAROLINE: (LAUGHS) ...the sensual swish of a woman in pearls as she turns her head to say (SILLY VOICE) *Is there an interval? Did you order the drinks?*

SOFI: (SHE LAUGHS, SCRATCHES HER BOTTOM, STANDS UP) God, it's not only being dead that makes me itch these days, I even get it sitting down. (BEAT) OK. We've talked about all the problems, all the awful things about acting. Why do we do it then?

CAROLINE: You saw what I did just now. (SHE POINTS TO THE SPOT) I had to pick up that picture. And it wasn't vanity. No, I've got hundreds of them stuck in cupboards upstairs. But I can't stand to see anything just lying on the floor. I may *live* with a man who gets drunk and snores and drops crap all over the place, but I need *neatness*. And *meaning*. (BEAT) That's why I'm an actress.

SOFI: Yes, I think I understand. You look for patterns. A script with a shape to it. Dialogue with a certain rhythm. (BEAT) So what else does an actress need?

CAROLINE: She needs the rehearsing and the learning of the lines because she wants to make sure there are no unpleasant surprises. So if she's married a bastard like a certain person I could name (SHE NODS IN STEVE'S

DIRECTION) she likes to know it well before the second act.

SOFI: (NODS) A woman like that, you can identify with.

CAROLINE: And she likes people to come in on cue, she likes to feel she can get a prompt when she needs one. (LOOKS AT STEVE) Hear me, Steve? Give us a prompt then.

STEVE TURNS IN HIS SLEEP, CONTINUES TO SNORE. SUDDENLY THE SOUND OF THE TOILET FLUSH

SOFI: I think Andy's done. Maybe I should…

SHE TURNS TOWARDS EXIT STAGE LEFT

CAROLINE: No, no! I'm sure he's left things clean and tidy. He looked a very clean young man. Most of the time.

SILENCE. THE WOMEN GAZE OFF STAGE LEFT, WAITING FOR ANDY. AFTER ABOUT A MINUTE, ENTER ANDY STAGE LEFT, ZIPPING HIS FLY, LOOKING SUBDUED AND SOBERED. SOFI WALKS ACROSS TO HIM AND HUGS HIM

SOFI: We were just talking about you. About how clean you are.

ANDY: (BEMUSED, RUBBING HIS FACE) Hell. Yes. I think I am.

SOFI: And about how great it is to be an actress. Or an actor.

ANDY: Oh, not for me. No. No. I couldn't do
that.

HE STUMBLES ON TO THE CHAIR VACATED BY
SOFI AND SITS DOWN. SHE GOES BEHIND THE
CHAIR AND LEANS AGAINST HIM
AFFECTIONATELY

ANDY: I'm just grateful I'm a bloody writer.
(BEAT) I admire actors, don't think I don't. My
dad always wanted to be an actor.

CAROLINE: Will I have heard of him?

ANDY: I said *wanted* to be. He never really
made it. (BEAT) His day job was selling
upholstery. He was doing walk-ons part-time,
but all it did was show him how good he was.
What was it he used to say? (BEAT) *You'd be
surprised, the number of people who can't take
the simplest direction, like open a door, sit
down, pick up a spoon, the number of people
who can't remember two lines together.*

CAROLINE: How'd he get the walk-ons? I'm always
interested in that sort of thing.

SOFI: Go on, Andy, tell her. (TO CAROLINE)
Gosh. It's a lovely story.

ANDY: He and my mum went to Butlin's in
Skegness with us kids, only I think it was called
Funcoast World in those days. Butlins were re-
branding. Anyway, he won the talent
competition.

CAROLINE: Butlins? That sounds very working
class.

ANDY: That's right. When people know I've been to Winchester, they all think I must have been born with a silver spoon. But it's not true. I got a scholarship.

CAROLINE: Clever boy.

SOFI: *I* think so.

ANDY: Right. My dad. He went on to win the national heat – well, he came *second* in the national, won a weekend for one in Cleethorpes. Really. He used to joke the *first* prize was only a *morning* in Cleethorpes. (BEAT) Anyway, the act he did at Butlin's, he played the piano, did impressions: Liberace, Bobby Crush, even Les Dawson! People nobody's heard of these days. (BEAT) And then he started doing the working men's clubs. Some of these clubs didn't even have a piano. (BEAT) *Can't you do it on the Hammond?* they'd ask. He used to say he was the only man who ever played the Warsaw Concerto on an organ!

SOFI: He was great, Andy's dad. I think that's what made me fall in love with him, hearing about his dad.

ANDY: Most nights my dad died. The club secretary would come backstage afterwards and say: *You're very good, you know, but you're a bit too sophisticated.* My dad used to say: *Any comedian who didn't say bum was an intellectual to these people.*

CAROLINE: So what happened?

ANDY: He started going in for TV quiz shows, I mean as a contestant. He thought it was a way of

getting his face known. He did *Mr and Mrs*, with
my mum. He did *Double Your Money*, *The
Golden Shot*, *Three-Two-One*. Made a fair bit
out of prize money too.

CAROLINE: That must have pleased your mum.

ANDY: It did a bit. But she hated going on *Mr
and Mrs*. That's why she left him.

SOFI: Tell Caroline what happened next.

ANDY: He had to give up on the quizzes
because of the walk-ons. He'd got an Equity
card through doing the clubs. He'd been writing
around to everywhere and suddenly, for no
reason, he started getting them: *Coronation
Street*, *Last of the Summer Wine*, even *Minder*.
Every little bit helped.

SOFI: But then people started writing in…

ANDY: …saying it wasn't fair that a TV actor
should be doing these quizzes when it should be
your ordinary man in the street who hasn't been
specially trained to walk straight and talk in
sentences. And I suppose they're right really.
Look at Reality TV. Half the fun is seeing
people trip up over the knickers on the floor.
(BEAT) So that was the end of that. He said he
was only ever himself when he was performing.

SOFI: *I'm* like that.

ANDY: But then he got offered a promotion in
upholstery. The management side. So it was
goodbye to the dream of stardom.

SOFI: *I* could never give it up.

ANDY :   Hell. All I know is it's the actors who have to speak the lines, and if there's a used condom thrown from the stalls, it's the actor who gets it. Not me. I can sit in the dress circle and pretend I'm part of the audience. *Nothing to do with me, mate!* (BEAT) Not that I've done any theatre. I'm just grateful I've got TV. Oh yes. Big budgets, real locations, production values.

SOFI: Our student stuff never had production values, but at least we tried. The director use to go down the road to Sofa City or Chair World or Pouffe Planet and say: *Lend us some of your stuff and we'll put your name in the programme.* And the people in the shop are only too eager to oblige.

CAROLINE: Advertising, you see? Advertising makes the world go round. That's what Steve would say, anyway.

SHE LEANS ACROSS TO STEVE

CAROLINE: You *would* say that, wouldn't you, Steve?

STEVE RESPONDS WITH MORE SNORING AND WRITHING

SOFI: We once did a production of (THINKS) one of Alan Ayckbourn's. (BEAT) And we all had to sit on a sofa and it still had the plastic wrapping on it. Plastic wrapping!

ANDY   Well if that's not a metaphor for bloody theatre...!

SOFI: No, no, that's not the full picture. It's not. That's just the downside. But there's an upside too.

CAROLINE: (SARCASTICALLY) Tell us about it.

SOFI: You know what I think about being an actress? It's not just having to take your top off and coming out of the toilets when Vera Duckworth's having a funny turn. And doing naff love scenes with a man who's just eaten garlic bread. It can be an escape. You can say: Tonight, I'm going to be beautiful. Tonight I'm going to be brave. Tonight I'm going to be powerful. Tragic. Noble. Tonight I'm going to be *loved*.

SUDDENLY CAROLINE STARTS TO CRY. SHE TAKES A HANDKERCHIEF FROM HER HANDBAG

SOFI: (HORRIFIED) What have I said?

CAROLINE: *Going to be loved!* Hah! (BEAT) It's not *you*. Honestly. (BEAT) I said it was hard to cry. But in real life it's easy. I find I'm doing it all the time. (BLOWS HER NOSE) He's called Edward. He's a lot younger than me. He's playing Caulfield in *Funeral Games*. Most people don't remember the play. It was on ITV.

ANDY: Oh, I still remember ITV.

CAROLINE: People don't think it'll last.

ANDY: How long are you booked in for?

CAROLINE: No, I mean Edward and me. People don't think it will last because of the age thing. And because it's bloody Bradford. (BEAT) And because it's *actors*. We're always mistaking the make-believe for real life.

SOFI: Oh, come on! If you really know your part and love it, then you get a feel for the way things are going to turn out. You have to take a chance that you won't be wrong about the ending.

CAROLINE: (SHE GETS UP AND WALKS ACROSS TO STEVE) You hear that, Steve? No. You don't hear that, do you? You're still dreaming whisky dreams. When I look at my pictures I think: *Who is it*? But I'm not really asking: *Who is it*? I know who I am. I'm the lying, adulterous bitch you ended up married to. That's what you always call me, isn't it? And that's what you always wanted me to say!

SHE TURNS AWAY FROM STEVE AND WIPES HER EYES AGAIN. SUDDENLY STEVE'S EYES OPEN WIDE AND HE STARES AT HER. HE LEAPS OUT OF THE CHAIR AND HOLDS HIS ARMS LIKE A CROSS

STEVE: Confession! Confession! (HE GRABS HER VIOLENTLY BY THE WRIST)

CAROLINE: (TRYING TO BREAK AWAY) Oh fuck, fuck! You *weren't* asleep!

STEVE: (CLUTCHING HER WRIST, MIMICKING HER VOICE) *You weren't asleep*! (REVERTS TO OWN VOICE) What a terrible line! It's just the sort of thing an actress *would* say. I'll forget about the fuck bit, the bad language. I won't be commenting on that. (BEAT) I mean, look at you!

SOFI: (BRAVELY RUSHING ACROSS TO
HIM) Let go! Leave her alone!

STEVE LETS GO OF CAROLINE'S WRIST. HE
TURNS TO ANDY AND SOFI

STEVE: And you, the audience! (BEAT) This is
the big climax. You both knew I wasn't *really*
asleep. You knew I'd suddenly come awake.
Suddenly surprise you. You sit here, listening to
this bitch shoot her mouth off and you're
thinking: *she's got a nasty surprise coming*!
You're all waiting to see what happens next.
Like some Alsatian lying under the table.
Salivating. That's what you are. Pavlov's dogs.
Waiting for the juicy bits.

ANDY: (BELATEDLY LEAPING TO HIS
FEET) Hell. Leave *us* out of it! And leave *her*
alone too!

STEVE: (LOOKING AT HIM IN SURPRISE)
What? What did you say? (RAISES HIS FIST)
What did you say, Mr Writer? Mr Eco-trash?
Little Sir Eco?

CAROLINE: (RUBBING HER WRIST) He said:
leave me alone!

STEVE: (LAUGHS) But look at them, just look!
They're just a typical audience! They're waiting
for me to beat you up. That's what they want. A
bit of sex and violence. (TO ANDY AND SOFI)
Why can't you get a life of your own? Why
can't you have your own sex and violence?

CAROLINE: (TO STEVE): You're so stupid! You're
just a failed playwright.

STEVE: And you're a typical actress! A bit-part actress!

CAROLINE: You strut about the stage shouting out the lines you wrote, the lines you think are so bloody wonderful...!

STEVE: Well, I don't say *wonderful*. But I do say they're not bad. Look at these two.
(INDICATES SOFI AND ANDY) I had them going a bit. I had their attention.

CAROLINE: And you *need* that, don't you? You need an audience! And you hate the fact that you need them! You think they're beneath you because they come and watch. But if you ever think you've lost them, you get scared, terrified. You're like a little boy behind the sofa, watching *Dr Who* on the telly.

STEVE: At least I've got integrity. At least I don't have to shag a bunch of actors. Oh, I've never met an actor who ever stopped acting. Not for a bloody minute.

CAROLINE: And I've never met a writer yet who wasn't tasting his own words every time he opened his mouth, thinking: *oh, that's not bad, I might use that.* Or worse still, *other people's* lines. Somebody in a pub says something that's half decent, and I see your nose twitch and your little piggy eyes narrow. And I think: *He's going to steal that. You watch out, mate, because he's going to steal your line. And you'll get nothing out of it, not even a thank you.*

SOFI: (IMPRESSED) Gosh. I know what you mean.

ANDY: Oh come on, that's not fair.

STEVE: (DISCOMFITED) I *don't* steal other people's lines.

CAROLINE: You do!

STEVE: Don't!

CAROLINE: Do!

STEVE: Don't!

CAROLINE: (TO ANDY AND SOFI) Do you see what he's doing? Do you? He's forcing me to do these staccato one-word things, these one-liners, to pretend he can write dialogue instead of bloody monologues.

STEVE: I'm not!

CAROLINE: Are!

STEVE: Not!

CAROLINE: Are!

SOFI: And she *didn't* think you were asleep, Mr Clever Clogs! (BEAT) Well, I don't think she was ever quite sure.

CAROLINE: (TO STEVE) When I think about our marriage, I feel like I've read the script so many times, and it's something *you've* written, dashed it off to meet a deadline like you do for your ads. And I don't like it. I don't like the ending for a start. And I'm going to change it. (BEAT) So don't go thinking I'm stupid. Don't go thinking I thought you were asleep. I was *acting* that I thought you were asleep.

STEVE: That's crap. That's the worst line yet! Stop it! I never wrote that line. (TO ANDY AND SOFI) Really, I never wrote that line!

CAROLINE: It's improvisation. That's what we actors do from time to time.

STEVE: (CRESTFALLEN) Well, improvisation is not a practice I've ever condoned. Not in *this* marriage.

CAROLINE: Let me tell you, Mister Writer: I've always got the edge on you. That's what lets actors win. Because whatever words you want to put in my mouth, I can change them. I can do that. I can just say whatever comes into my head and there's nothing you can do about it. I've got my audience and they love me.

STEVE: They don't love *you.* (TO ANDY AND SOFI) *You* don't love her, do you? (TO CAROLINE) They love the *writing.* The sound of the words. The only time they'd even take a second look at you is if you took your top off. (TO ANDY AND SOFI) You *don't* love her, do you? Come on, let's hear it from you.

CAROLINE: (TO ANDY AND SOFI) You *do* love me, don't you? (BEAT) *Somebody's* got to love me! (BEAT, THEN TO STEVE) Is that what you want me to do then? Take my top off?

STEVE: Yeah. Come on. Give them what they want. Give them what they've paid to see. *You're* the bit part actress. Let's see the bits.

CAROLINE: *You're* the writer. But if I do, it'll show
    your writing up for what it is.

SHE STARTS TO PULL DOWN HER SHOULDER
STRAPS

SOFI: No. no! *I'll* do it! I'm *younger* than you!

SHE ALSO STARTS TO PULL DOWN HER
SHOULDER STRAPS

CAROLINE: (ANGRILY TO SOFI) Well. Thanks.

ANDY: (TO SOFI) You will *not*!

SOFI: Why not? I've been thinking about it a
    lot lately. I've had offers.

ANDY: Oh yes. I'm sure you've had offers. And
    I'm sure they were a lot better than this one.
    Look, I'm your (BEAT) partner. I'm not going
    to have you strip off in front of strangers unless
    it's a damn good deal, commensurate with the
    embarrassment involved.

STEVE: (REACHING OUT TO CAROLINE)
    Stop. Hold on. (BEAT) I told you I'm not that
    sort of writer. (BEAT) I told you. I don't say
    my lines are wonderful but... (BEAT) Look.
    This Edward...

CAROLINE: Yes?

STEVE: Do you really love him? (BEAT) We
    are, after all, civilised people. We're both
    grown-ups. People have the odd fling now and
    again. Especially when they're apart. Like
    actors. Especially actors. It doesn't count on
    location. That's what Sam Goldwyn said.

SOFI: I don't think Sam Goldwyn ever went to Bradford.

CAROLINE: (TO STEVE) I don't know. I don't know what I feel. Edward's… (BEAT) Like I said, he's a lot younger than me. People don't think it'll last. And I've noticed myself trying to hide my nipples under the duvet. So I don't know if I'll be able to take it seriously for much longer.

STEVE: Do you take *me* seriously?

CAROLINE: When it's *you*, I still get that feeling. (BEAT) Unless it's one of your off days. One of your *drunk* days.

STEVE: Come to bed?

ANDY: (LOUDLY) Oh my God! What is this?

CAROLINE: Is that in your script then? Did you plan it? Did you write it up beforehand?

ANDY: (TO SOFI) I don't think we should stay.

SOFI: (INQUISITIVE) I don't know. There may be lessons to be learned.

ANDY: Like what?

SOFI: Like presentation. Staging. Lighting effects.

ANDY: Lighting effects, my arse!

STEVE: (TO CAROLINE) Not on stage. Not in front of *them*, the audience. (INDICATES

ANDY AND SOFI) I told you, I'm not that sort
of writer. And I'd never really ask you to take
your top off. (BEAT) Not on stage, I mean.

CAROLINE: No sex or violence then? No jealousy?

STEVE: I think we should try for a happy ending.

SOFI: What about the audience?

STEVE: (TO ANDY AND SOFI) I think you two
deserve a happy ending too.

ANDY: That's the real problem with being a
writer, isn't it? People say they're up for a bit of
realism, but all they want in the end is a
feelgood experience.

STEVE AND CAROLINE KISS IN A PASSIONATE,
LINGERING WAY. THEN:

CAROLINE: Ok then. (SHE TAKES STEVE'S
HAND, ADDRESSES ANDY AND SOFI)
Well, that's it. It's time to say goodnight.
Modesty demands. (BEAT) Can I call you a
taxi?

SOFI: Why don't you just call me stupid? I
didn't believe you really thought of us as some
kind of audience. I thought we might be (BEAT)
friends or something.

CAROLINE: I don't think we ever have friends. Not
actors and writers.

STEVE: Writers and actors.

THEY KISS AGAIN, THEN:

STEVE: (SHAMEFACED TO ANDY AND
                SOFI) But I do want to apologise to you. I'm
                sorry if it's been a bit of an anti-climax. As a
                writer, I always find the endings are the hardest
                bits.

TOGETHER, GAZING INTO EACH OTHER'S EYES,
CAROLINE AND STEVE WALK SLOWLY STAGE
LEFT AS IF ABOUT TO EXIT. THEN CAROLINE
BREAKS AWAY AND TURNS BACK

CAROLINE: (TO ANDY AND SOFI) Oh come on!
                Look on the bright side! You got a free drink out
                of it. (SHE GOES OVER TO THE TABLE
                AND PICKS UP THE PHONE BOOK) Alpha
                Taxis. They're very reliable. Look. I've written
                the number at the top of the page.

STEVE: Come on then.

CAROLINE: Come on yourself.

THEY EXIT SLOWLY STAGE LEFT, HOLDING
HANDS

ANDY: (CALLING AFTER THEM
                SARCASTICALLY) Well, thanks very much!

SOFI: Gosh. What do you think that was
                supposed to be? Some sort of (BEAT)
                masterclass in misery?

ANDY: I feel like the couple in a horror film
                who get stranded in Transylvania and end up
                staying the night at the vampire's castle. (BEAT)
                But *we're* not staying! Not *this* time! We're re-
                writing the whole bloody script!

HE OPENS THE PHONE BOOK, STUDIES IT,
TAKES OUT HIS MOBILE, RINGS THE NUMBER

SOFI: (VERY ANGRY NOW) Not staying? I
should *hope* we're not staying! I hope we never
see them again. (BEAT) I can't believe that
people turn out this way. I can't believe that we
might…

ANDY: What?

SOFI: Turn out like… (HORRIFIED) We
won't, will we?

ANDY: Turn into vampires? Of course not.
We've got too much (BEAT) good sense.
(BEAT) I'm really furious. I thought at least I
could get a tampon commercial.

SOFI: What?

ANDY: (INTO PHONE) Hello, hi there, hello,
Alpha Taxis?

THEN:

CAROLINE: (DISEMBODIED VOICE, SCARED
AND ANGRY) Steve, I don't care what you
think! I don't care any more!

STEVE: (DISEMBODIED VOICE) You bitch,
Caroline! You lying, cheating bitch!

SILENCE AGAIN. THEN SOUND OF LOUD SLAP
FOLLOWED BY WOMAN'S HIGH-PITCHED
SQUEAL. ANDY AND SOFI LOOK AT EACH
OTHER HORRIFIED. BRIEF SILENCE.

ANDY: (INTO PHONE) No. There's no trouble, mate. Don't worry. Honest. (BEAT) Hell. It's only a bloody sound effect.

LIGHTS DIM

END

About the author

Michael Yates was successively reporter and film critic on the Sheffield Star newspaper, and also worked as a subeditor for the Bradford Telegraph & Argus and the Huddersfield Examiner.

He taught playwriting at Harrogate Theatre and creative writing for the Workers Educational Association, and in 2010 was Writer in Residence in Bradford Schools.

He has had short stories published in magazines and anthologies and won short story prizes from the Jersey Arts Centre, The Armagh Writers Festival, the Wolds Words Festival and The Writers & Artists Yearbook.

Michael has been Poet in Residence in Whitby, in Wakefield Hospitals and at Wakefield Cathedral, and has published three volumes of verse.

A dozen of Michael's plays have been performed in the North of England, including Manchester, Wakefield, Leeds and Bradford. *Sunday Afternoon Again* was chosen for the Write Now Liverpool Drama Festival in 2012. *Life Sentence* won the Stanley Arnold Trophy at the Sheffield One-Act Play Festival in 2009. And *The Bronte Boy* toured West Yorkshire in 2011 and a new production was commissioned by the Bronte Society for their international AGM weekend in Haworth last year.

Also by Michael Yates in Nettle Books

The Bronte Boy

Young Branwell Bronte, who once ruled an imaginary world, is now a man, grown mad trying to cope with the real one. Having failed as a poet and painter, as doomed in love as he is in literature, he slips ever more quickly down the road of drink, drugs and despair. His loving father Patrick and talented sister Charlotte fight a last-ditch stand for his salvation, but it is Branwell's sinister friend, gravedigger John Brown, who threatens to have the last word in this ultimately terrifying take on the brilliant family we have read so much about and all thought we knew so well. Full text of the play plus cast lists.

Paperback. 80 pages. £6. **ISBN** 978-0-9561513-1-5

Short Shorts Volume 1

Three one-act plays: *Life Sentence*, in which a vengeful wife threatens her faithless husband with an axe unless he confesses all; *Till my Eyes Bleed* in which nerdy Mel holds a wake for his dead pal Adrian unaware of the true relationshiop between Adrian and Mel's wife Beatrice; and *Sunday Afternoon Again* in which eight-year-old Lenny worries about his parents fighting – and the wicked witch who lives next door.

Paperback. 115 pages. £6. **ISBN** 978-0-9561513-3-9

Also in Nettle Books

Flying with a Broken Wing

By Sat Mehta

Flying with a Broken Wing tells the true story of a boy growing up in India in turbulent times.

Sat Mehta was five years old when he and his family became refugees, caught up in the biggest migration in modern history at the time of Independence. His home was destroyed, his uncle murdered. Once very wealthy farmers, the Mehtas became destitute.

Later, Sat suffered a broken arm, complications set in and amputation seemed inevitable. As he lay in hospital, a world famous surgeon, Professor Robert Roaf, strode onto the ward, choosing "hopeless cases" to help. Sat got a second chance.

The gratitude he felt for the great man's skill shaped the rest of Sat's life. He qualified as a doctor and arrived in England, where he has lived and worked for 30 years.

He says of his life: "It is a story of a disappearing world, sadhus, snakes and baking sun, monkeys, monsoons and riot and murder. As a boy, I saw it all."

Paperback. 180 pages. £10. **ISBN** 978-0-9561513-2-2

www.ingramcontent.com/pod-product-compliance
Lightning Source LLC
Chambersburg PA
CBHW051847170626
46807CB00003B/1390